LEFT TURNS

12 TALES OF RASH DECISIONS AND BEAUTIFUL MISTAKES

Button
HALL

CONTENTS

While pursuing a dangerous man through the streets of Victorian London, a midwife must battle her own conscience in order to avenge the assault of a woman in her care—and fulfill the rumors of her namesake.

Resisting the guardians who are trying to turn her into a thief, a young Irish girl struggles to keep herself and the children in her life fed in the slums of turn-of-the-century New York City.

When a childhood buddy resurfaces and offers him a part in the heist of the century, a lonely young dishwasher finds out who his real friends are.

When a socially invisible high school girl impulsively steals her neighbor's laundry, she ultimately brings down a bully and finally feels seen by her classmates.

Looking to escape a boring summer, a sixteen-year-old girl takes a job on a locked men's ward of the local state psychiatric hospital and learns more about life than she anticipated.

When her colleagues stage an intervention to pull her out of self-doubt, a young woman is thrust into a false identity, leading her to a deeper understanding of her true self.

Lorin Oberweger

An elementary school science teacher has all the answers for their students but is at a loss to explain why their true love seems to be slipping away.

INTRODUCTION
LORIN OBERWEGER

BRONZE AGE NEWLYWEDS. A midwife in Victorian London. A college professor with impostor syndrome.

The characters, settings, and genres featured in this story collection could hardly be more different. But as with any great work of short fiction, the protagonists have in common the fact that they've come upon some crucible moment—a critical inflection point—in their lives, and afterward, nothing will be the same.

That's what we want from our fiction: characters at compelling life crossroads where the decisions they make will alter the course before them in grand and unexpected ways. And while we want things to work out for those characters, we not-so-secretly love when they make a mess of things. We keep reading in the hope that they'll untangle themselves from their often-self-inflicted chaos, but it's the tangle that keeps us turning pages.

We love our characters' humanity, their wounds, their "rash decisions and beautiful mistakes" as the subtitle offers. And we love to see them emerge from the tumult in an altered state. In doing so, we—as readers—are altered, too. That's the promise of great fiction and the reason we come to the page over and over again. These stories deliver that and more.

Speaking of crucible moments, on May 31, 2018, a small group of writers gathered in Davenport, Florida for the launch of a new two-year writing program: Story Lab. A few years later, another set of writers would gather for the same purpose. They came from different locations, different backgrounds, and different levels of experience. Some had already been well-published. Some were just starting on that path.

Their personalities were different, as you'd expect, but they also had much in common. Not only were they gifted writers, hand-selected from a couple-hundred applicants to participate in the Lab, but they were all driven to be their best. They were sometimes intense and exacting, hard on themselves, but always willing to put in the effort, to push themselves and the boundaries of their craft, to rise to challenges set before them, and to *grow*. And they were kind and generous with one another, creating connections and forging ongoing communities—one result of which is this project.

I don't know if they know, even now, how talented and special they are or how much they grew during our years of working together. But I trust you'll see what I see in these pages. Fun, extraordinary, stirring, and—most of all—human stories from exceptional writers with so much to offer.

Enjoy.

THE KNIFE

KATHERINE LONGSHORE

While pursuing a dangerous man through the streets of Victorian London, a midwife must battle her own conscience in order to avenge the assault of a woman in her care—and fulfill the rumors of her namesake.

Katherine Longshore is a bookseller, book coach, and author of four historical fiction novels for young adults. In her non-book-related hours, she loves to travel, eat tasty food, and spend time in the outdoors with her family and dogs.

PLAYLIST

One Way or Another — **Blondie**
Respect — **Aretha Franklin**
O The Wind and the Rain — **Peggy Seeger**
Red Right Hand — **Nick Cave and the Bad Seeds**

Scan to listen at buttonhall.com/books/left-turns

ukey is still screaming when I walk away. You may think me unfeeling, but no matter what comes next, I'm not a monster. I close my ears. I imagine myself like Lot's wife, telling myself I cannot turn.

My undoing is that I know I'm not running from evil, despite what the clergy and the good people of the city might say.

I'm moving towards it. Following after it on purpose.

So, when the screaming stops, I do, too.

The other girls have crowded around her, churning the dust of the courtyard into mud. She's still crying, her face corrugated by pain and shame. She doesn't curse the man who did this to her. The only word I hear is the hoarse refrain of *Mama, mama, mama*. The hot metallic smell of fresh blood mixes with the constant terror-and-shit reek of the meat market at Smithfield.

The smell of my childhood.

Everything within me wants to go back to her, tend to her—put arnica on her bruises, feverfew for the torn skin. Chamomile tea for her nerves. My mother taught me all of it, but it's a plaster, daubed on, not meant to last.

Jenny meets my eye, holds my fear, my anger, my hesitation in her own, then lifts her chin abruptly.

"Go," she mouths, adding something else I can't quite read, something about Polly.

We can't let this man get away with it. He thinks he already has.

That's why he stopped halfway across the courtyard with that slow, sharking smile. That's why he pulled out that flat stack of notes—notes he retrieved from the Bank, not an hour ago and used to cajole Sukey into trusting him *just this last time*. A bundle of white fivers he fanned himself with, knowing nobody here in Pigeon Yard would stop him or steal from him, because he is Louis Miller. Because he works for the Crown, for Victoria herself, he is untouchable.

He didn't even leave thruppence behind for poor Sukey, with her left arm hanging loose and her petticoats torn. This man has done this before, here and elsewhere. He will do it again without thinking twice. Let's be honest—he'll do it without thinking once.

So, I follow him. We'll show him who the shark is.

I slip off down Cock Lane. He's nearly at St. Barts, where the crowds grow thicker and I might lose him, so I hurry. I memorize his clothes, his manner, his movements. Though Louis Miller is of middling height and not particularly handsome, he is vain, and his clothes reflect it. His thick, dark overcoat with the nipped-in waist, the gray silk top hat, trousers with a stripe a bit too bold, making a statement. His slender cane swings gratingly out of rhythm with his stride.

He doesn't turn round, doesn't know he's being followed. Wouldn't actually know it if he looked. I've never been remarkable, and now I'm through the Change, I don't even have youth to make me noticeable. I grew up ashamed of my plainness, of the way a man's gaze would land and not linger, not see anything to make him look again. It pained me. Now, I hope it serves me well.

A shout behind me draws his eye in my direction. I swallow, keep moving. If I look away, if I stop, I might raise suspicion. I wonder—I hope, briefly—that he will feel a prickle of premonition when he sees my face and know his fate. It will be like a vision in a story, when you see your reckoning coming. I hold my breath.

He doesn't appear to see me at all—a plain figure in simple skirts and gray hair starting to thin, the strays pressing stickily to my neck. Being a woman of a certain age is the best disguise in the world. I could creep up on him, slit his throat, and vanish before he hit the ground.

No one ever suspects the woman, that's what makes it so easy,

Polly said, as she and Jenny conjured this plan together, so many years ago. She has always done this. She has always been the one. I try to swallow a thick bite of grief and gag on it.

Polly is gone, and it's my turn now.

I continue to watch Louis Miller. He pauses at Pye Corner, and I don't slow my pace. Could I do it now? My hand begins to tremble, so I clutch it around the folding knife in my pocket, wishing away the trickle of sweat that pools along the top of my corset.

I tell myself there are too many people on Giltspur Street, passersby who will come to his aid. The hospital at St. Barts is so close that if I get it wrong, the surgeons could save him. He stands solidly in the gap of sunlight between buildings, his head turned to one side as if someone's about to draw his portrait. Unmoving.

Maybe I'll keep walking all the way to the new Postman's Park, use that tiny patch of green to catch my breath. To think on where I came from, and not this path I'm on. My mother raised me to save lives. Children. Cripples. Mothers and babies. I fear I am actually the opposite. That in order to save the lives of Sukey and Lenya and the other women like them—like us—I must become what Polly was.

A plunderer, predacious—a silent, fatal blade.

I come to the end of Cock Lane, not an arms' span from Louis Miller, close enough to see a thin crust of shaving foam left behind his ear. He turns right, and I take one more step toward the road, toward a different life—I can almost smell the cut grass at the Park.

Instead, I turn, and there is Louis Miller, admiring himself in the windows of the White Hart, not a care in the world, not in a hurry for anything. He knows no one will make him pay for what he's done.

When I start toward him, he sees me, his face quizzical like he recognizes me or my expression. I can't keep going. I can't even pretend. So I turn swiftly around to the Fortune of War, that dodgy old public house beneath the statue of the Golden Boy.

I stop, trying to hold back my breath, which comes in great gusts like a bellows. The windows of the pub are begrimed, as if trying to hide what's happened there, keep it in the shadows.

Not that long ago, the body snatchers—the Resurrection Men, as they called themselves—used the back rooms to display corpses to the surgeon-teachers at St. Barts. No one asked where they came from and no one told. Donation, the graveyard, the knocking shop around the corner.

More than one girl from the Yard ended up in those back-rooms. I remember my mother standing outside, shouting at the doctors striding brazenly by me, clinging to her hand. Shouting about the kind, cow-faced girl abandoned by her farmer father one market day and left to navigate the streets of London on her own, until she found the Yard, and the girls, and my mother who tended to them with her herbs and her poultices and her skills with needle and thread.

To the surgeons, Alice was nothing but a penniless prosti-tute. Who she was didn't matter to them. She wasn't human, even before they got their hands on her.

My heart stoppers my breathing, and I look up to the fat little golden boy overlooking Giltspur Street. He's watched all the comings and goings since before I was born. When I asked who he was, my father peered at the plaque on the wall and said something about gluttony and the Great Fire, whatever that was. I was just a girl, never taught to read the plaque myself, so to me, the Golden Boy remains a pudgy little cherub with big balls (far too large for a child his age), and the serious expression of a man on the watch.

What he's watching for, I've no clue, because he's certainly not watching out for us.

My father didn't either, not really. Tiger Brown, who worked in the prison when he arrived in London, a warder. After five years, he moved to Smithfield to become a butcher instead, coming home covered in blood instead of desperation. He kept his head down, as blinkered as the animals he slaughtered.

I take a huge breath in through my nostrils, and regret it immediately. The surgeons use the wall beneath the Golden Boy as a urinal for some wretched reason known only to tosspots and men. I pivot on my toes, ready to give chase again. Following in my mother's footsteps, in Polly's, fighting for those who need it most.

Louis Miller is not to be seen.

Giltspur is busy with hats and coats, men of the hospital, the market, the Old Bailey. Louis Miller could have gone into the White Hart to celebrate his cruelty. He could have turned north, toward the market, to pinch his rents from the stallholders. Or south, toward Newgate and his offices of the law.

I've missed my chance, too cautious, too afraid. With my hesitation, my hawing, I have failed. The faint glow of relief at my reprieve is bitter comfort. It is cowardice, a weakness as irresistible as a drunkard's need for ale.

I clench my hands together, close my eyes. I do not want to be a weak and feeble woman. I want to be a force to be reckoned with. I want to be the fear that stops a man like Louis Miller.

I CAN FIND HIM.

I know these streets. I grew up on them. *Here, Lucy, let Mrs. Clarke down Shoe Lane know we've got Suffolk lamb. Lucy, girl, I need you to take this tonic to Alma Crook's daughter in the square.* This was long before the National Education League and Lord Ripon and the other toffs decided the poor needed the three R's, so my school was the bloody gutters and back-alley apothecaries of Smithfield. Between Fleet Street and St. Paul's, a warren of streets devoted to butchery and God, newspapers and the infirm, and direct in the center of it all, Newgate Prison. All human life is here and no one knows these streets better than I.

Thinking hard about Louis Miller, I remember the way he flashed his fivers. He's already been to collect his rents, been to the Bank. I have a good idea which way he's gone.

I turn right towards Newgate.

My parents were from outside the City. My father from Thurrock, one of the Boy Soldiers in the war against Napoleon, paid to leave his parish at the age of twelve. Da felt hemmed in by the walls, the streets. Felt a prisoner of them. Mam loved the city. There were no herbs and hedges growing for her to gather ingredients for her potions, but she would shrug and say *you can buy anything in London.*

Even people.

Mam loved a place where she could be invisible, disappear entirely, if she so pleased. Back in Colney Heath, *her* mam was watched. Sometimes spat upon. The Methodists avoided her completely, barked her for a witch. A woman with a life of her own was thought obscene. In London, no one knew who Mam was. She was, in a sense, free.

I hurry past Old Mags, sprawled on the path, his legs so screwed and bent he needs his niece's child to come and collect him every day. He touches two fingers to the crease of his cap as I pass and I send him a wish. I can't stop, not to drop a coin or a kind word, the bitter sense of purpose eating me thin. I still can't see that shiny hat band, that smart, smugly stride. I have to find him.

I hurry toward the church of St. Sepulchre-without-Newgate, called the Old Bailey in the children's rhyme, forever linked with the Courts and the prison across the street. Today, the bells are silent—no weddings, no funerals. No executions to announce.

Not officially.

I spot Louis Miller, as if conjured. He likes to think himself unblemished, and therefore keeps aloof from the crush. He has cleared himself a path, or perhaps it clears for him.

He passes Peter in his rags, there by the back gate of the church. Those who don't know Peter call him the Dancing Man, due to his bouncing walk and flapping arms. Louis Miller swerves, as if the stutters are contagious.

Up by the door of the Viaduct Tavern, a little girl crouches in the street, picking up browned and dimpled apples into the hammock of her pinafore, tears cutting lines in the dirt on her face. Louis Miller slows a little, a hitch in his stride. He's watching her, I can see the tip of his hat, the angle of his neck. He sees her—he actually sees her and her struggle, and for a moment, I am viciously angry. If he acts with kindness, it will ruin everything.

Then I'm awash with blessed relief, because I will be able to turn back. Not even Polly could hold me accountable.

The man merely rocks his weight to his left foot, and kicks an apple from beneath the girl's fingers, sending it spinning and spitting juice and rot all the way into the crowds of Newgate Street. It splatters on the skirts of a laundry maid, who shrieks and drops her basket, causing a domino reaction of stops and jolts in the foot traffic.

A crowd can turn on you when you get in the way, Da used to tell me. He hated them, Ma loved them, and they're all I've ever known. I hadn't set foot across the river until I met Mackie. Beguiling, handsome, a teller of tales. He had the charm of a magic amulet—or a snake—and I straightaway fell in love when he turned that charm on me, skinny as a blackthorn wand and wide-eyed as the calves dragged to market. Married me, aged sixteen, promising to show me the world.

My parents balked a bit, Da questioning that Mackie wanted to be called Captain. *Captain of what, I want to know. We were private soldiers, and none of us ever became an officer.*

They liked him even less when he married Polly, too, but that turned out to be my saving grace. *She* was my saving grace. Because of Polly, I truly see the world. Because of Mackie, I know how to navigate it.

I PRESS a hapenny into the palm of the little girl and pause at the corner, where Louis Miller slows for the sluggardly assemblage along Newgate Street. Somewhere, across the road by the prison, an organ grinder is playing an old murder ballad, *The Twa Sisters*. That will cheer the inmates, I'm sure.

Polly used to sing it to me—mostly in jest—the story of a pair of jealous sisters, ending in drowning and bones being used to make a harp. She was older than I, the daughter of a man who'd been running rackets around Fleet for years, a kingpin who stole money from beggars and rooked the local shopkeepers. He had the ear of the jailer and the courts, and could wrangle a murder conviction for an innocent, if he so wanted.

I was terrified of her.

A pirate queen, she was, a real criminal mastermind, smarter than her father and Mackie put together. *Twa Sisters* aside, she taught me the only way women can make their way in this world is to take care of each other, every one of us. Men may show us jealousy, wrath, indifference. They may tell us it's our fault, as well. If we are to survive, we can't wreak that on each other.

Mackie wandered, but me and Polly, we stayed together.

Louis Miller walks right out into the street without looking—maybe he'll do this job for me—his passage hampered by an omnibus drawn by a knackered-looking horse, breathing heavily as it pauses, waiting for the apple-spattered maid to gather her basket.

A cabriolet thunders by, stirring dust and scattering pedestrians. To my disappointment, Louis Miller escapes unscathed except for the feculence on his shoes.

The maid fares worse, tipped back on her arse, the contents of her basket scattered around her. Louis Miller throws a half-hearted curse at the cab driver, reserving the lions' share of his vitriol for who he sees as the real cause of the melee. He grinds a white shirt beneath his heel, spouting abuse, and pushes the maid almost beneath the wheels of the ambling omnibus.

I launch myself across the street. Polly would have marched right up to Louis Miller and sent him into the street as well, shouting, "Eat dirt!" and standing with one boot on his back like the figurehead on a Spanish galleon.

Mackie would drink with him in the back of a tavern until the publican found him relieved of his faculties, his money, and his ale. Potentially his trousers.

I cannot focus on Louis Miller and his deeds right now. Not with this girl literally getting spit upon by the rest of the crowd, emboldened by one man's spite.

I help the maid up, get her to the side of the road and out of danger. I pick the gravel from her palms and use my handkerchief to wipe the horse shit from her cheek. She begins to cry again, not from fear, from the kindness. I think I will take her to my father's old butcher's shop, where they still know me, and get her some beef tea, and maybe discern what else is the matter, and help her—just her. That has to be enough. I have to believe helping one person can make a better world as much as ridding it of another can.

Polly disagreed with me, right up to the day her tumor killed her, and probably beyond. *You have to dispose of the trash*, she would say, *before you can clean the house.*

I'm not Polly, so maybe this is my purpose. She didn't believe in heaven or any kind of afterlife, so I can't ask her if maybe helping is enough—every act a small pebble in a big pond, to be sure, but those ripples reach far.

"Thank you," the girl says in a voice quiet in tone and loud with rural Irish, sincere in its gratitude.

"You all right?" I ask.

All the others on the street ignore us both. The men in their hats and coats, busy with purpose, their eyes on the money, the market, the conquest, and not on what's around them. The women, aware, avoid eye contact. They try not to see us, because we should be invisible. The poor, the literally downtrodden.

"Fine," she says, straightening. "I'm Mary. Mary Finneran." She brushes at her skirts—an act of inestimable optimism if there ever was one. Then she smiles, broadly, revealing a gap between her front teeth and a chipped canine. I can't help but smile back.

I hesitate to give my name. Polly had two rules.

1. Don't let them see you.

2. Never let them know your name.

Polly is not here.

"Lucy," I say, and give my married name. "Lucy Macheath."

She sucks in a breath, fast and short.

"Macheath, like Captain Macheath?" she asks, her eyes wide.

I kick myself. The image my husband's name conjures up is someone who gives no quarter, who takes what he wants and cares not for who it affects. A man not dissimilar to Louis Miller, just in a different milieu. I have terrified this girl for no reason.

"I—" I start to say, when she cuts me off with a fierce embrace, throwing me into confusion.

"I can't believe it's you," she says passionately, pulling away to study me. "I can't believe it's true! I've heard about Captain

Macheath, of course. Everyone has. The men are full of stories of bloodshed and thievery, and can't agree on whether he rapes the women or pimps them. But it's true, isn't it?"

I stare at her, voiceless. That's the story we want, the story we've cultivated. In truth, Mackie is a pussycat. A teller of tales, the ones you believe. He makes his stories—our stories—more real than the truth. Stories of cutthroat highwaymen and vengeful pirates, terrorizing law-abiding citizens from the back alleys around Newgate Prison.

It serves my purpose to use our husband's name, on occasion, so people don't give me grief. Everyone thinks to be afraid of him.

Except this girl. My heart lifts at her delight. It loosens with each step that takes Louis Miller further away from the fate I'm meant to deliver him. The burden I wasn't supposed to take on.

"The stories in the women's quarters," the maid gushes, "and down the courtyard on washing day. All the girls know. All the old gammers. The stories they tell, they're all about his wife, and how *she* runs the racket, how they bring her the men that crossed her and ask, *do we kill them now or kill them later?*"

She says this last with the relish of a highwayman, herself.

"That's not quite—" I don't know how to finish that sentence.

"But her name is Polly."

The grief fills my heart and my head with a roaring that will never cease. In three months it hasn't come close. Polly wanted the credit, the acclaim.

"They say she travels with a witch," the girl says, carefully. "Is that you?"

I am and I am not. All the words for women—maid, whore, gammer, hag, crone, *witch*—none of them true, all of them hiding the person within. I heal with herbs, I feed an unruly black cat, and I disappear before you know I'm there. Some would say that's proof enough I'm a witch.

"You don't want your secret to come out." She hugs me again, and whispers in my ear, her breath hot on the back of my neck. "You have no worries with me. I won't tell. I want you to know, though, we are all proud of you. We all want to *be* you. You give us hope, you and Polly." She laughs, and presses a finger to the corner of her eye, where tears have sprung.

"There should be a song about you, shouldn't there?" she asks. "The organ grinder can play it outside the prison and put the fear of God into them all. Swift as a shark and as silent, not a drop of blood on your gloves." She grins.

For a moment, I imagine it, having every ear tuned to my melody. To strike fear into men's hearts when they realize who I am. Who Polly was.

Then I laugh. Because Mackie would take the song over and make it about him.

***

"I must go," the maid says, suddenly, her face white as a new gravestone. "My master is there at the church." She snatches up the basket of filthy shirts and backs into the crowd.

I turn to see the pious retreat from the church with their slow steps and smug faces, utterly aware of the wickedness around them, and yet pretending they are immune. Two of them —and the priest—I've seen down the Yard. The priest prefers Lenya, who shouts like a demon, but the deacon, like Louis Miller, goes for Sukey, who is quiet and simple and doesn't fight back.

I don't know which is this maid's master, but her terror is of more than reprimand over dirty shirts.

"Lucy!"

I turn at the shout—a joyous one. The maid waves a brave hand.

"Thank you!" and she disappears.

Something shifts in me, then. I helped that maid rise from the ground, that is all. I have to *earn* the thanks she gives.

I take a chance and start off down the Old Bailey. Here, between the tall buildings, the road is murky, steeped in mud and other fluids, the stink of wet rising coldly, the walls dark with it. Fewer people here, and Louis not among them. I've taken too long, lost my way. The failure hits hard and clings bad as muck.

I stop in the middle of the street, my hem soaking up the piss and the mud, and I want to howl. For Sukey. For the other girls. For Mary Finneran. For the women whose bodies used to find their way by bad luck and misadventure into the hands of the teacher-surgeons of St. Barts, for my mother, for myself.

What I'm planning to do—if I have the courage when the moment comes—is only a temporary measure. There's always another man, around the corner, at the end of the day.

It's enough to crush a person.

It crushed Polly. All the men who couldn't see what she was worth. All the men who treated her—and me, and the others— like we'd brought it on ourselves for the grave misdeed of being born a woman.

I continue on down each dead-ending alley. Green Arbour Court. Bishop's Court. St. George's Court. Not there. Not there. Not there.

Thank you. The trust in those two words. The hope. That's what Polly started.

I turn down Limeburner Lane, flagging, losing hope. Just then the sun comes out—a single ray splitting the clouds like the hand of God. I no longer believe in any white beardy God in the sky, so I choose to believe it's Polly. It lights up where Lime- burner meets Seacoal Lane, and there it is, a dove-gray hat with a blue-black band, shining for a single moment before the clouds snap shut like a door.

I want to run, to keep him in my sights, but that's the surest way to call attention to myself. No man can resist a woman running. He wants either to protect or pursue, and I need neither.

So I walk, quicker than I normally would, as unobtrusively as possible.

For minutes, I catch glimpses of him up ahead of me, and I see him turn down Seacoal toward the Bell Savage Public House —or where it used to be—and my heart thumps against my whalebone stays, because Seacoal is narrow and dark, and since they built the viaduct few use it. It's not safe for a woman alone.

It's not safe for Louis Miller, either.

My skirts drag with damp, my palms sweat. My fingers slip on the folded knife in my pocket. Can I open it quick enough?

Can I, in the moment, actually use it?

<hr>

THE ALLEY NARROWS as it approaches Fleet Street. This is my chance.

I quicken my pace, sorely aware of of my own footsteps on the cobbles, the sound hurried and anxious. I've set something in motion I cannot stop, a boulder down a winter hill shorn of wheat. Except what I've set in motion is myself. Who knows what might get crushed along the way.

Then he turns and my feet stop as quick as hitting a wall, nearly toppling the rest of me. I squeeze my fists in my skirts, open my mouth, and no sound comes out.

He tips his head to one side, the top hat rakish. Infuriating.

"Do I know you?" he asks, half a laugh in his voice, because why would he? Why would he recognize me as the woman he's seen twice before in the span of an hour?

My ribs contract, squeezing tight beneath my corset, holding in the fear, keeping it contained.

It cannot contain my rage.

"You know my—" I stop. Choke. *My daughter, my sister, my friend.* "Sukey."

Saying her name gives me strength. I'm doing this for her. For all of them. I take a step closer. If I can keep that in mind. If I can keep myself on the path to which I've been set. If I can—

"Who?" Louis Miller still wears that amused expression, as though I'm something silly he's come across. An anecdote he will relay to his club.

Sukey is not an anecdote.

"Sukey," I tell him. I take another step. "You've just left her in Pigeon Yard. Her arm may be broken." And worse.

He frowns, then, with a quick glance up and down the alley to see who might overhear.

"Oh," he drawls when he realizes we are alone. "The tawdry little *whore.*"

It rises within me, the fury. Generations of it. My grandmother, shunned as a witch, and *her* grandmother, burned for one. My mother, laughed at by the surgeons, even as she saved the life of a new mother they had left as a lost cause. My daughters, sisters, friends—the *whores*—used, abused, and forgotten.

And Polly.

Out of habit, I swallow down wrath like a stone. Deference, capitulation, compromise—they are a debilitating addiction, and one I cannot afford. Not now. Ashamed, I struggle to resummon the ferocity I need, but I am hamstrung by my own witless desire that he somehow be worth saving.

"Do you not care?" I shout, but it's faulty, flawed. It comes out a question rather than a rebuke.

"Care for what, old woman?" He is fully dismissive from his hat to his gloves. "Why should I care what's left in the gutter?"

The question. The half-smile. The eyebrow. This man I've hunted through London's streets so obviously on the verge of rolling his eyes and expelling a tactless cough in scorn.

I see myself through his eyes. Hag, harpy, harridan, witch. All true. His vision of me absolves me of the customs required of a mere woman. I feel something new rising within me. Something more than rage. Something better.

Pride.

"You should care," I say, taking one step closer. Close enough I have to lift my chin to meet his eye. "We are all of us in the gutter."

Only some of us are looking up instead of down. Which is worse—picking pockets or rash speculation? Selling your body, or selling the drug that removes your mind and kills you slowly? What's murdering a man, compared to employing one in the mines or the mills or the penal colonies of Australia? They are all the same. I may not be better than Louis Miller, but I am certainly no worse. Mankind commits all manner of wickedness.

"You can't see any different, because you're nothing, and have no way of rising up," he says. "You and your Sukey and the rest of your whores. You don't matter. You could disappear off the face of the earth and no one would know."

Perhaps I should feel the truth of this, but I don't. "I suppose the same can't be said of you."

"When I die, it will be written in the *Times.*"

I'll never know, as I couldn't read it if I cared to find this man, this Louis Miller, mourned in print for all to see. Telling everyone, everywhere, what a good man he was, and how much he will be missed.

Which stories last longer, which tell the bigger truth? The ones in the paper, or the ones told down in the sculleries and at the wash houses? I feel the smooth knife in my pocket, ready. Finally ready.

"Sukey matters," I say. "She's the child of a seamstress and laborer, a man who helped build the Crystal Palace. She can turn her hand at anything—from stitching roses on her petticoats to mending the kitchen table when..."

I stop talking. The table broke when someone like Louis Miller threw Lenya onto it and it collapsed beneath her.

"What is she to you, then?" He takes the final step that closes the gap between us and leers down at me. I can smell the bear fat and quinine in his mustache wax. "Something you don't have the word for? In your ignorance, you know it's shameful, but you do it, anyway? Is it jealousy that brings you here, then?"

I bite my tongue. I know the word. The words. I know all of them, as I've heard them all before. Me and Polly both. As if the only thing a woman can be—if she's not fucking every man available, or at least thinking about it—is an invert.

How silly men are, as if those are the only options. If they think there is no room for friendship in their lives—no room for the kind of brotherhood that comes from sharing laughter, sharing sorrow, sharing birth and death, a room, a bed, a toilet, a secret—then I should feel sorry for them, for him. In another life, maybe I would.

Not today.

I flick the worn handle on my knife blade, not taking my eyes from his, but the soft, silky click of it draws his gaze and for the first time, he wavers. Swallows.

"What do you want?" he asks, still thinking he can escape.

"I want you to leave Pigeon Yard."

He smirks, lifts his hands, and raises his face to the narrow ribbon of sky above us. "I have left Pigeon Yard."

"I want you never to come back."

I could do it now.

"Fine, fine." He steps back, casually, and I fear I've missed my chance. He's like a man about to pull his pocket watch, check the time. *Have we concluded our business?*

"I want the money you owe Sukey."

I'm losing my nerve. He's too far, too big. The cane gripped in his hand could easily knock the knife from mine, or crack my skull, break my arm.

He shrugs, drags the bundle of notes from his inside pocket, and leafs through it, taunting me with what he's got and I haven't. Setting his cane aside, he pulls out a coin from his trouser pocket, tosses it to the mud at my feet, and laughs. He doesn't believe me capable.

He doesn't know me.

Quick as a cat, I crush the coin beneath my boot, and he's suddenly with his back against the slimy brick wall, nowhere to go and no leverage, the point of my knife at his throat.

Most men fear a blade to the heart, and most men go for it. I know the heart is too easy to get wrong. I know the surest way to kill him. I see the blood pulsing there.

My father was a butcher, after all.

"Who are you?" Louis Miller asks. His Adam's apple bobs against the blade, and he flinches.

I am the daughter of Tiger Brown and his wife Elizabeth. I am a skivvy, a midwife, an herbalist, a wife, a woman, a witch. I am the song that keeps Polly Peachum's memory alive.

Louis opens his mouth as if he wants to say something, do something—anything—clever enough to get him out of this. But I'm done, here.

I speak over him, drowning him out, as so many men have done to us women for centuries past and for surely centuries more to come. "I'm the Knife."

I drive the blade home.

THE PICKPOCKET
LAURIE CALKHOVEN

Resisting the guardians who are trying to turn her into a thief, a young Irish girl struggles to keep herself and the children in her life fed in the slums of turn-of-the-century New York City.

Book coach and children's book author Laurie Calkhoven has published more than fifty books for children and teens ranging from early readers and funny chapter books to historical novels that bring the wacky facts of history to light. When she's not writing or reading, she can be found roaming around the museums, theaters, and parks of New York City. Visit her at lauriecalkhoven.com

---

PLAYLIST

McNally's Row of Flats — **Mick Moloney**
The Last Rose of Summer — **Celtic Woman**

Scan to listen at buttonhall.com/books/left-turns

ittle Sean kept his eyes glued to the lump on the other side of the dark basement. Except for the rise and fall of the man's chest with each loud snore, Mr. O'Brien didn't move. He was well and truly passed out.

"I'm going to do it," Little Sean whispered to his friend Birdie.

"You can't," she answered. "If he wakes up, you'll get a beating."

"We'll starve else," Little Sean said. "He's got more than a few coins in his purse, and we've got empty bellies. He won't miss the cost of a loaf of bread."

Even in the dark, Birdie could see the bruises from Little Sean's last beating. He'd gotten caught with his hand in a man's pocket and dropped the money as he raced away. It wasn't the man's shouts for the police that had angered Mr. O'Brien, nor the fact that the little boy almost ended up in the hands of the coppers. It was the dropped money that led to the thrashing. Mr. O'Brien set on the boy as soon as they got back to the basement. The memory of Little Sean's screams sent a shiver down Birdie's spine. He limped for two days, and the bruises on his face and arms had barely faded.

On the other side of her, Birdie heard Maureen, one of the O'Brien's five children, whimper in her sleep. They hadn't been fed more than a few bites of stale bread that day. The water from the pump outside smelled and tasted of the privies, but the little ones choked it down.

Birdie took a deep breath, trying to ignore the stench of the unwashed bodies around them. She sat up and straightened her shoulders. "I'll do it," she whispered.

"You can't, then *you'll* get a beating," Little Sean said.

"I won't. I won't wake him. And even if I do, he won't beat me as bad as he beats you. He's afraid of what my Da will do when I finally find him."

Little Sean opened his mouth to argue, but Birdie crept away before he could change her mind. She pressed her lips together and crawled across the basement hoping she wouldn't put her hand down on one of the rats or mice that came out at all times of day.

Slowly, quietly, she slunk to Mr. O'Brien's side and checked to make sure that he and the Mrs. were still dead to the world. It hadn't taken them long to discover how much cheaper strong drink was in New York City than it had been at home in Ireland. Mr. O'Brien spent freely on it, all the while marveling at the money he was saving. Drunken Saturday nights in Ireland turned into every night in New York City. While his children practically starved for want of food.

She hadn't liked the look of the family from the first second she laid eyes on them on the Liverpool docks. She and Mam had made their way there from Dublin where they were to catch a ship to join her Da and her brother Tommy in the City of New York. But Mam died suddenly the night before they were to set sail. Da and Tommy had saved for ever so long for those tickets, Dad laying bricks and Tommy selling *The New York Sun*. Birdie was desperate, tickets in hand, looking for a way for a lone girl of eleven to sail to America.

Seeing Mrs. O'Brien being ignored by her husband and struggling with five children gave Birdie the courage to ask to be taken on as a mother's helper. She handed over her ticket and Mam's besides to Mr. O'Brien and traveled under the O'Brien name. Da and Tommy would be waiting for her when the ship docked. Birdie was sure.

She had no idea how Mr. O'Brien planned to earn his living in New York until she was trapped in the steerage section of the ship with them. Little Sean—an orphan they had taken in—was being trained in the way of picking pockets, the other children being too young. Mr. O'Brien was an expert when he wasn't drunk, and even a sober Mrs. O'Brien could waltz through a crowd and come back with a change purse or three.

Birdie had stepped onto New York City soil, planning to run into Da's and Tommy's arms. But they weren't there. They weren't anywhere, despite all of Birdie's attempts to find them. For a full month she looked for them everywhere, checked in weekly at the Irish Aid Society, and asked every newsboy she saw if he knew a Tommy Doyle.

With no other kin in New York, Birdie stayed with the O'Briens. They lived in the basement of the worst rookery in the Five Points, the worst slum in all of New York City. With most of their stolen coins going to drink, Birdie was expected to do more than mind their five little ones. Unless she learned to pick pockets like Little Sean, she was on the edge of being thrown out to survive alone on the streets.

She thought about evenings at home, before Da and Tommy left for America. Family songs and stories around the fire in their little cottage. Mam's good cooking. And a whole village that had watched over Birdie and Tommy as they grew.

How will I face any of them ever again? How will I face Da if he finds out I've been earning me bread by stealing from others?

She shook off that worry. *I'll not be able to face them at all if I die from hunger.*

Fingers trembling, she reached toward Mr. O'Brien's pocket. He had always lectured them to be quick when stealing someone's purse, but she was too frightened to make haste. Praying her shaking hand wouldn't wake him, she slipped her fingers slowly, slowly, slowly into his pocket. She could feel them vibrating against his leg. *Sure, he'll grab my arm the way the man on the street grabbed Little Sean.*

But she couldn't turn back and risk Little Sean doing the deed himself. She kept reaching for Mr. O'Brien's change purse. Finally, her fingers grasped it.

Just then, Mr. O' Brien rolled over with a huge snore, trapping Birdie's hand and his purse beneath him.

She froze. Little Sean gasped. The ruckus he would cause if he cried out and woke the others would earn them a beating from both the Mr. and the Mrs. So she made a game of it, flapping her free hand in front of her nose in an exaggerated attempt to wave away the stink of the man's breath. The stench did truly make her want to recoil with each of his exhales.

Little Sean pressed a hand over his mouth. It was too dark for Birdie to tell if he was holding in laughter or screams.

Mr. O'Brien's snore was loud enough to wake his wife.

Mrs. O'Brien rolled over, slit her eyes, and mumbled for Birdie to take the baby. "I need me rest," she slurred.

The baby was, in fact, asleep between Little Sean and Maureen, along with the O'Brien's three hungry boys.

"Yes, Ma'am," Birdie whispered. "I've got her. You have a good rest now."

The Mrs. rolled over with a snort.

Birdie closed her eyes and concentrated on breathing without making a sound. There was nothing to do but wait until Mr. O'Brien rolled over. The longer that took, the more likely it was that someone would wake up and ask her what she was doing, unless . . .

Birdie pulled a piece of dirty lace off her cuff and used it to tickle the man's nose. He rolled over again, this time with a thunderous fart. Miraculously, no one stirred.

Birdie mimed dying of the stink so that Little Sean wouldn't panic. She could just make out his shoulders shaking with laughter. Then she claimed her prize—his change purse. It was heavier than she expected. She took out a bit of money and considered dropping the purse at his side instead of slipping it back into his pocket. But that might make him suspicious. She risked slipping it back into his trousers, nearly sure that he'd been too drunk when he passed out to remember how much money he had.

I guess this makes me a thief, she thought. *Sure, I've been fightin' this ever since we landed in this awful City of New York. But I'm doing it to fill his babes' bellies, not just me own.*

It was Mr. O'Brien's own fault. He was the one who, over and over, tried to train Birdie to pick pockets. Seeing how hard life was in this terrible city and how little most people had, Birdie hated the idea of taking from those who would suffer from the loss. No matter how hard Mr. O'Brien tried to teach her, Birdie made sure to make him believe she'd get caught every time—jostling his arm too hard, banging his leg when she reached into his pocket, and anything else she could think of to give herself away.

Until now.

She shook off that thought and crawled back to Little Sean with Mr. O'Brien's coins in hand. They crept upstairs and out onto the street. Birdie half expected a vengeful Mr. O'Brien to come up behind them like a demon from a story, but he didn't. They slumped against the side of the building, catching their breath.

Aside from some drunks stumbling around, the street was quiet. There were no pushcarts or the calls of vendors, no begging children, and no grownups rushing past them. Even the saloons were subdued, most of their patrons passed out or on the verge of it. But Birdie remembered an all-night eatery a couple of streets away.

As soon as she got far enough away from the Rookery that she felt safe, Birdie was overcome with relief and then laughter. That set off Little Sean. Each time they looked at each other they burst into another howl of glee until the tears streamed down their cheeks and they had to hold onto a building to remain standing.

They had finally caught their breath when Little Sean mimicked Mr. O'Brien's ear-splitting fart, and they doubled over again.

Birdie's stomach hurt from the joy of it mixed in with the hunger. It had been a long time since she had laughed until she cried. "C'mon," she said when the giggles had slowed enough for her to talk. "First we eat, then we buy food for the little ones."

An hour later, they had eaten their fill of corned beef and cabbage—their first hot food in days. The waiter made them show him their coins before he would bring the food. When he finally did, they had to resist the urge to shove it down as quickly as possible or it would all come up again. They chewed and swallowed, chewed and swallowed, not stopping to talk or even look at anything other than the plates in front of them. Birdie knew it probably wasn't tasty. If she was fed properly it wouldn't even have been appetizing, but at that moment it seemed like the finest meal Birdie had ever eaten.

After they had finished and been shooed out of the eatery, she and Little Sean leaned against each other in an abandoned doorway and struggled to stay awake while they waited for push-cart vendors to begin selling their wares and the bakeries to open.

"What'll we tell 'em, Birdie?" Little Sean asked, stifling a yawn, "about where we got the eats?"

"We woke up hungry, you picked a drunk's pocket, and we used the money to buy food," Birdie said. "The lads won't be crying because their stomachs are empty. And Mr. O'Brien will be thinking he spent more on rum and whiskey than he remembers."

She started to chuckle again at the thought of picking his pocket, and Little Sean joined in, resting his head on her shoulder. He dropped off to sleep, a smile stretched across his face.

In her worst moments, Birdie let herself think that Da and Tommy had found out that she had left Mam alone in Liverpool with no priest to speak over her body. How else to explain that they weren't there to meet her? But she shook off that thought as she always did and concentrated on staying alive long enough to find them.

Now I'll have to tell them I've become a thief, too. But I'm not giving up. I'm going to find them and make them forgive me. I'll live a life that doesn't mean stealing from other folks.

Out of habit, Birdie asked every newsboy who ran past if he knew of an Irish lad named Tommy Doyle who sold the *New York Sun*. None did. None ever did.

Finally, the sun rose above the sooty tenement buildings, all of them crammed full with families trying to stay alive in this place. She nudged Little Sean awake. A baker tried to pawn off stale bread for the price of newly baked, but Birdie knew better and demanded fresh. Pushcart vendors eyed them suspiciously and made Birdie pay before they turned over their wares muttering about the dirty Irish.

On her way back to the rookery, she realized why. She caught sight of her reflection in the window of a second-hand shop—her hair dirty and matted, her face covered in the muck of the basement floor, her dress—so pretty when she left Ireland—torn, dirty, and already too small. She looked like all of the other street kids in the Five Points.

Will Da and Tommy even recognize me if they see me now? I barely recognize meself.

She and Little Sean entered the basement to find the children sobbing and the grownups—thankfully—still asleep.

Maureen raised her arms with a whine and Birdie ran to her.

"We thought you'd gone," Paddy said with a snuffle, wiping his face on his sleeve.

"Leave this fine castle, and all you fine princes and princess-es?" Birdie said. "Sure, me and Little Sean have been out seeing to the business of the day."

Little Sean proudly brandished four whole sausages to be divided among them along with two loaves of bread. The three boys pounced, and Birdie had to practically fight to keep Maureen's share out of their hands. She split the toddler's sausage in two, giving one piece to Little Sean for later, and pulled out a piece of the soft center of a loaf for Mary Margaret, the baby, to suck on.

"Don't eat too fast, now," she warned the boys. "And take bites. Don't swallow them whole."

The boys danced about waving their sausages between bites, using them like pirate swords. But they were quickly swallowed, followed by the bread, and some stale water from a bucket in the corner.

It was hard to keep the boys quiet now. Cormac, at six years of age, was the ringleader, telling his younger brothers about all the grand feasts they would eat when they were older and could pick every pocket in New York. "We'll sit at the grandest tables and call for cakes and sausages," he declared.

"And pork and beans!" Paddy added.

The fact that the boys couldn't imagine a future that didn't involve stealing made Birdie sad, but this morning she had to smile at their boasting. "Don't forget corned beef and cabbage now," she said, "and a fine Irish stew."

"What's this ruckus then when I'm trying to sleep?" Mrs. O'Brien clawed her way up the wall until she was standing. She saw the bread in Maureen's hand and reached out to take it, but Maureen answered with a scream.

"Did not one of you save something for your poor old Mam?" Mrs. O'Brien asked.

The boys were cowed for a moment, eyeing each other. But Little Sean stepped up with two more loaves and an apple.

Mrs. O'Brien dropped one of the loaves on Mr. O'Brien's chest and quickly had to shoo away a rat.

"Haven't you had enough now?" she muttered, noticing the hopeful look on the boys' faces. She turned her back on them and gobbled down half the loaf.

"We had sausages!" four-year-old James announced.

The woman growled. "Sausages for beggars and only bread for those that take care of 'em?"

Bread and whiskey, Birdie thought. *And rum. And thieving isn't the same as hard, honest work.* "He's telling tales," Birdie said quickly. "We've had no sausages, only bread. Right, boys?"

"No sausages," Cormac yelled, giving James a smack. "No sausages. Right Paddy?"

"Right," Paddy agreed. "No sausages."

The children eyed each other, their lips twitching.

"Where'd the food come from, then?" Mrs. O'Brien asked. "You steal it?"

"We was hungry, Birdie and me," Little Sean said. "I picked a drunk's pocket, and we bought bread for everybody."

Little Sean gazed at Birdie and soon they were roaring with laughter again. The younger children joined in, even though they had no idea why they were laughing. Even the baby gurgled.

Mrs. O'Brien stomped out back toward the privies, grumbling. It wasn't long before she was back and snoring again. It was up to Birdie to try and find some milk for Mary Margaret with the two pennies she had left.

***

"Nice and easy now," Mr. O'Brien said when Birdie approached him that afternoon. "Nice and easy."

Birdie stuck her hand into his pocket to snatch his change purse, being sure to brush up against him and pinch his leg instead of his purse.

"Dang it, lass," Mr. O'Brien roared. He raised his fist.

Birdie flinched, but that seemed to appease him enough that he didn't strike her—this time.

"Why do you think God gave you them long, skinny fingers if not to pick a man's pocket without him noticing? Try again."

"Yes, sir," Birdie muttered. "I'm doing me best."

"Your best ain't good enough, girlie," he shouted.

It wasn't her best. Hadn't she proved last night that she could pick his pocket easy? But stealing was wrong, and she wasn't having it. She made a new rule for herself–if the little ones were starving, she'd find a way to feed them. Even if it meant stealing. But only then. Sure, she was going to face her own Da with her head high.

She tried again and jostled Mr. O'Brien again. He shook his head with disgust. "Even that dolt of a boy can do better'n that," he said, pointing to Little Sean.

Birdie stared at her feet, pretending to be sorry, but she remembered picking his pocket last night and it was all she could do not to laugh.

"Don't you smirk, girl," Mr. O'Brien growled. "Yer gonna earn your keep, if you're gonna live under me roof."

Birdie looked around the dark basement room they shared with another family in a building filled to the brim with people in crumbling room after crumbling room. People of all sorts. Most of them drunk. All of them hopeless. Children ran wild, stole, begged for bread. At least once a day there was a fight and most mornings a dead body was carried out and left on the curb.

"It's a roof, girlie, and better'n what you'd find on your own," he grumbled. "There's plenty out on those streets will ask you to do a lot more than pick a pocket." His voice got louder. "Some'll even pay for a girl like you."

Birdie winced. He had never threatened to sell her before. She did know that there were worse fates for girls out on the streets. She could only hope that the Mrs.'s need for a mother's helper outweighed his need for a thief.

"Now you." Mr. O'Brien pointed at Little Sean. "You show her how it's done."

Little Sean ambled toward Mr. O'Brien, lightly brushing his shoulder against him as he walked past. Then he glided by Mrs. O'Brien. When he turned, he held two change purses.

"That's how it's done, girlie. Now try again."

I'll try again, Birdie told herself. *But it won't be a pickpocket that finds Da and Tommy. I'll survive somehow without stealing.*

She did try again. And again. Each time meeting Mr. O'Brien's fury with a penitent look.

He'd make her keep trying. And she'd keep failing.

Every single time.

DREAM CATCHER
MARK FIGLOZZI

When a childhood buddy resurfaces and offers him a part in the heist of the century, a lonely young dishwasher finds out who his real friends are.

Mark Figlozzi was born in a small town in northern New York, where there are more cows than people. He studied writing at Oberlin, screenwriting in LA, and is the creative director of a design agency in Seattle.

PLAYLIST

The Tales of Lee Scoresby — **Lorne Balfe**
Fools Gold — **The Stone Roses**
Sky Fits Heaven — **Madonna**
Fields of Fire — **Big Country**
Sabotage — **Beastie Boys**
It's All Too Much — **The Beatles**
Angel — **Massive Attack**
Keep the Car Running — **Arcade Fire**
Unstoppable — **Sia**
Just When You're Thinkin' Things Over - **The Charlatans**
The Dream Police — **David Byrne**

Scan to listen at buttonhall.com/books/left-turns

"'ll lay my cards on the table," Johnny says.

We're speeding across the moonlit bay in the back of a hoverboat. No one's driving, because Johnny programmed the route before we left. So we sit back on cold vinyl seats drinking a couple of beers, like we're out for a joyride.

And it should be kind of joyous, seeing Johnny again after all this time. But it's cold. And something's not sitting right with me, only I can't put my finger on it.

"End of August," Johnny says, leaning in, "I run into this guy I know— he's real connected in the underworld, and he's drunk. So I get him talking. And tells me there's trouble in the underworld." Johnny lowers his voice, looking around. "Apparently the prawn king — Molek hisself — has managed to steal a *military grade dreamcatcher*."

"Whoa!" I say, hoping I sound the right amount of impressed. Not *too* impressed, like some country bumpkin. But not *not* impressed, like someone who doesn't even know what a dreamcatcher is.

"No shit!" says Johnny. He's practically yelling above the rush of wind and the hiss of water against the bottom of the hoverboat. "If the prawn king actually figures out a way to use this thing, it could shake up the whole balance of power in the gulf!"

I wouldn't dare yell like that, for fear someone would hear us. But nobody's anywhere nearby, not for miles and miles across the bay. So maybe Johnny knows what he's doing. I hope so.

"Now, the prawn king's rivals ain't standing still," he says. "Molek wants to smuggle the dreamcatcher to Mexico, but he can't get it across the border with the other gangs on edge. So he's holed himself up on an island compound. Heavily-guarded. An island *fortress*."

The waves are huge out here. *Ocean* waves, heaving and tossing. More water than I've ever seen, and Johnny's got the hoverboat going crazy fast. We're zipping across the surface almost without touching it, except when the big waves lift up higher than its AI can plan for, and a swell of salt water thuds against the bottom of the hoverboat, which is *wicked* hot. The water snaps and hisses and steams, and sprays me in the face, and each time it happens, I think we hit a rock and we're gonna blow to pieces. We don't, but I'm wet and shivering, now. Somehow Johnny, right beside me on the seat, stays dry.

"The prawn king's island has three defenses." He holds up three fingers on his right hand. "But my guy told me the fix for all of them!"

The water below the boat is deep black. You can't see the bottom. Can't even see beneath the surface. There's no guessing how far down it goes. I pull back from the edge and grip the bench, trying to find something that's not moving to focus my eyes on. My guts squirm like a pile of eels.

"You listening, Glen?" Johnny doesn't wait for me to answer. "It's gonna be dark by the time we get there. We'll slow down when we enter that cove; we're gonna be running real low. We glide in. Right against the water. Quiet as a duck. We wait in the swamp grass a bit. Then, when I give the signal, *this is how it's gonna go down.*"

THE GUARDS

"The island's divided into twelve zones, going around like the numbers on a clock. In four of the zones, there's guard stations. That's the first thing we gotta look out for: the guards." Johnny takes the last swig of beer and tosses the empty can over his shoulder.

"But I got a fix for them. I got the skinny. At two minutes to midnight, my guy says there's a change of shift. Four fresh guards fan out from the main compound up that hill, and head across the rockfield. They line up like sheep, one at each station. When they're all in place, they take the stations offline. The sleepy guard comes out, and the fresh guard goes in. But here's the thing."

Now Johnny laughs, and pulls out a smokestick. He pops the end in his mouth and shuts his eyes. Johnny's not worried about anything. That's why he's such a great guy to do this with. That's why I'm so lucky he found me after all these years, and brought me along for his idea. Johnny's always had a lot of confidence. He's a confidence man, I guess.

"For the swing shift," he says, "it's quittin' time. These guys are tired and they're dumbasses. Minimum wage guys — like you and me, right? At quittin' time, what are they gonna do? Shoot the shit, Glen! So during the shift change, my guy says they're real distracted.

"And even when they are payin' attention, the only thing those guards are good for, is if one of them sees anything out of the ordinary, he will press a big red button in his booth — to alert the main compound. And *that*, my friend, is where the sentinels come in."

THE SENTINELS

"The sentinels are *thing two*." He holds up two fingers. "We do *not* want to wake the sentinels. They're the heart of the prawn king's defense. You know what a sentinel is?"

He glances at me and I squirm a minute. "A fancy word for guard?"

Johnny stops talking. He takes the smokestick out of his mouth and holds it between his fingers like people used to hold tobacco cigarettes. It's waxy and has Johnny's teeth marks on it. I know I said something stupid. Shouldn't have answered at all. Should have kept my mouth shut, but I'm shaky all over, jittery and twitching from the cold and the wet, and I wasn't thinking clear. I don't know how Johnny keeps so calm.

"A sentinel," says Johnny, "is a lethal, fast-moving, black-market crawler-drone."

"Oh, a crawler drone."

"Fast moving. My guy says the prawn king's got at least a dozen sentinels. Even Molek can't afford to run them all the time, so that's why I say *don't wake'em up.*"

I chug my beer, trying to catch up with Johnny. Warm beer and the rocking boat don't sit well together and it disturbs the eels in my gut. I'm gonna be sick.

"Remember that, Glen. Don't wake 'em up. Now, that takes us to *thing three.*"

MOTION SENSORS AND KILL LIGHTS

"The third thing you gotta look out for is motion sensors: Ultra-violet surveillance. They're always on, watching in the dark. Fanning out from that central compound in twelve kill zones. Any movement in your kill zone — poke your head over that ridge or knock a pebble loose — and your zone lights up with the *kill light.*"

"Kill light?" This works up the eels again.

"You know about kill light, right? Glen? The sentinels are built on old military AI — even the black market models. So they all have one big weakness: they can't see for shit. They can't see in the dark, or even in ordinary daylight. They can only focus on one thing at a time, and they can only see where the kill light shines! That's *treaty* shit, Glen. Everybody knows that."

Did I know that? I almost get the feeling Johnny's *trying* to scare me. Like maybe he gets a thrill telling me all the things that could make us dead. And I'm trying to hide it, but the damn shaking is giving me away, and I wish Johnny would mention the shaking, so I can explain: It's the cold, that's all. And the rocking of the boat. I'm not used to all this water.

"Don't worry so much. As long as you don't get seen by the guards or the motion sensors, there'll be no kill light shining — and you're safe from the sentinels. And don't worry about that motion sensor either — because it's the changing of the guards, remember? And those boys are all walking across the rockfield at the same time. Do you know what that means, Glen? You figure it out?"

"What's it mean, Johnny?"

"It means the motion sensors are switched off — from two minutes to midnight till two after! So you got a whole *four minutes* to get yourself from the shore, across the rocky field and up to the main compound without anybody seeing you!"

And now he cracks that Johnny smile, and everything's okay again.

Johnny can do that. He has that look. His eyes go real narrow when he smiles like that, but there's a sparkle that shines through. The sparkle tells you there's a center to the universe, a bright place where great ideas get made real. Where adventures can happen. A special place, where a guy can make something of himself, no matter where he comes from. And Johnny's it. Johnny's the place.

Me and Johnny both grew up in Albedo around the same time. Before he texted me Thursday morning, I hadn't seen him in six years, but we picked up right where we left off. No hard feelings. I hadn't seen anybody from Albedo that whole time, not even Ray or Eduardo.

I'd been living in a rent-a-room, washing dishes at the Hi-Spot off Route 12, and trying to earn my lunch each day. It ain't bad work. You get into a zone and it makes the days go by fast. Pez, the graybeard short order cook, says that once you settle into a groove, it goes the same way with years.

So I was partway through the breakfast shift. I dumped a heap of leftover eggs and syrup down the slop trough, and I had just slid the dirty crocks into the Ultraclean when a text came in.

Seeing Johnny's name on the screen, I felt years of sadness hit me like a dust storm I didn't even know was brewing. Like a cloud passing over the sun. It hit me harder than I would have thought. Living so far from home, I guess, I had built up an ache that was with me all the time. Like a creeping sadness I didn't even know I felt.

And then, getting that text from Johnny made the ache go away, for a minute. An ache I didn't even know I had.

Glen long time no see. Got an opportunity and I thought of you. Meet me?

I texted him back right away, then I waved at Pez and walked out of the Hi-Spot.

When you're with someone who knew way back when, you don't have to explain yourself. It's like there's a common language you can both fall back into. I wanted that again.

But meeting Johnny in the parking lot that night, things were different than I expected. Johnny smells different now. There's a scent like tar or day-old smoke on his clothes, and still I get a whiff of it now and then, even out here on the water. He never used to smell like that.

He looks different too. Past few days on the road, I've seen a joyless kind of hard edge to him that wasn't there before. And maybe now, in Johnny's boat, I'm feeling the ache of all those years come back, just a little.

"Glen," he says.

I shiver. The wind is getting real cold now. When we first got in the boat, and started across the bay, I could see the city lights on the shore. But now there's nothing but Johnny's face and the bottomless black sea and the howling wind and Johnny's strange new smell and a whole lot of empty nothing and I don't know how far down beneath the surface any of it goes. What choice does anyone really have?

"Earth to Glen."

"Hey, Johnny. What happens after?"

"So what you'll do is make your way — what's that, Glen? You say something?"

"I only was wondering what happens once we get the dream-catcher."

"Once we have ourselves a military-grade dreamcatcher? You asking what happens?"

"Yeah."

"Anything we want! For the rest of our lives."

"Yeah, but what I mean is—"

"You don't — you don't know what a dreamcatcher does, do you?" He stares at me, his mouth gaping. "Do you even know what it is?"

"Well—"

"Why did you even..." Johnny throws up his hands. "A dreamcatcher can do anything. Everything. Understand? With a dreamcatcher, you can make *anything* real."

"Like what?"

"Whatever you can think of. Use your head."

"Yeah but like, how does it—"

"I don't know how it works." Johnny turns away, exasperated. "Quantum manipulation, thought-energy fields, or some shit. I mean, you're the idea guy, right Glen?"

"Uh huh."

"So dream. Imagine your life!"

I think about that for a second. But it's been a long time and nothing really comes. I don't really have a whole list of ideas in my head these days. Besides, I find myself getting caught up on something.

"But Johnny," I say carefully. "Where are you gonna be?"

"Wherever the fuck my imagination—"

"I mean, while I'm crossing that rocky field, with the four off-duty guards? What are you doing at that time?"

"Oh!" He slaps me upside the head, like a brother would. Like a loving big brother. "Remember I told you we don't wanna see those *sentinels* coming out. We don't want the dumbass guards pressing their big, red buttons and alerting *those*. So to keep *you* safe, to make real sure, I'm gonna jam their signal."

"That's nice, Johnny."

"You bet. Now—"

"And how you gonna do that?"

"With this, loser!" He kicks the black and red duffel that's under my feet, that I've been tripping over the whole time. "The signal jammer, remember? That my guy gave me? The whole reason we're doing this? Now listen. When I jam that signal, this is what's gonna happen..."

And keeps on reciting the plan, running through every detail.

This is what's gonna happen, Johnny says. *This is how it'll go down.*

But now I'm thinking: *How do you know what will happen?*

* * *

ALBEDO WAS no place to be. We all knew that, growing up. Just a place to be from.

The rusted-out trailer where I grew up is just off the interstate. Out by exit 118, everything is flat dirt, dusty and hot. Some days the air doesn't move at all. You could sit and listen all summer, and you won't hear nothing but cars and locusts. Even the rattlesnakes just sit there, baking to leather.

Grass grew in the fallen-down barn behind our trailer, and a family of brown jackrabbits lived in that grass. They would freeze whenever you walked by. They were near invisible unless you could spot their big, brown eyes. Always open. Tiny hearts beating fast. Just a layer of soft fur between them and an eagle's talons.

Round sunset they'd gather to watch the highway, looking for a space between the trucks. Waiting for a chance to make a mad dash across hot asphalt to the grassfield on the other side. Why they didn't just live over there I'll never know. Take all their jackrabbit sisters and brothers and cousins and go. They could have.

A kid growing up in a place like Albedo will play with anyone. I had it better than most, maybe, with Ray and Eduardo. Ray had a ton of toy trucks, some rusted and some colorful. Most days after school, he let us play with him on the dirt mound out behind his house. Good old chubby Ray.

That dirt mound was an anthill of tunnels and holes and even some bridges and a sometimes swamp that was sometimes a lake. It was our village and our camp. We were cops and mayors, long haul truckers and short order cooks, robber bands and outlaw kings.

I guess I was the idea guy then. I'd look things over for a minute, then I'd show Ray and Eduardo what the trucks were gonna be up to that day. Round sunset, when Ray's mom called him in for dinner, the day's adventures would evaporate, just like that, and it was a pile of dirt again. Me and Eduardo had long walks home in opposite directions.

It must have been the end of ninth grade or the beginning of tenth when we first noticed Johnny around town. I don't know where he came from. Johnny was a senior, who wore a cool-guy jacket and chewed smokesticks. He knew how to buy whiskey and he claimed he could get girls to do anything he wanted.

Me and Roy and Eduardo still had mound-dirt under our fingernails. A bunch of ninth or tenth grade losers with no place to go. I don't know why he wasted his time with us. Maybe we were like charity for Johnny, or maybe he saw something in us we couldn't see in ourselves.

He came round when he wanted to cook something up. Sometimes he had a notion, and sometimes he wanted to see what we could come up with. If it was a good enough idea, well, maybe he'd join in.

In those days I used to scribble a whole mess of ideas on my yellow notepad, and keep it under my bed. I been scribbling my ideas in that notebook for years. Places we might go. Adventures we might some day have. Like anything would ever happen.

So one spring evening, Johnny came round looking for ideas, and I was ready. I casually suggested my lightning bugs idea, like it was something I just thought of. It was stupid, really. I don't know what he ever saw in it. But I took my shot.

Johnny shrugged and said, "Sure, let's do that."

I shrugged too like it was no big deal. My lightning bug idea from my idea notebook.

To get ready, me and Ray and Eduardo and Johnny waited around chewing on smokesticks and drinking cans of Zodka till the sun went down. And when Albedo was all tucked in for the night, us four crept down Pájaro Ridge through the old school playground. Johnny cut the chain link fence with a pair of wire-cutters, and we crawled through, into the lot where the city parked the school buses at night.

We popped a door open and climbed onto the first one. There was that old school bus smell, like when we were little. Rubber seats baked all day in the sun. We stood there inhaling — we were pretty drunk by then. Then I saw it, just like I remembered — there on the dash was the little metal switch to turn on the yellow school bus blinkers.

We switched them on, then we ran outside.

Those supernova lights were about bright enough to knock us drunk kids over. Two spots, like two blazing stars. We all looked up at those brilliant lights, scared, I guess, that they *were* gonna spark a wildfire in that dried up, scrubby parking lot. And then they shut off with a *click*.

And then one *click* later, they were on again.

On. And off. Day. And night. Repeat.

Johnny sniggered. We all started to laugh. But with that first school bus flashing like a beacon in the night, we knew our clock was ticking. That was part of the thrill of my idea. The ticking clock. That was why Johnny said yes.

So real quick, we split up, and ran around to all the buses, turning on all them yellow flashers. We hit all forty buses, just like in my yellow idea notebook.

The world was spinning now. But oh, what we made. It was like a whole field of fireflies, blinking and blazing and bumping against each other in a crazy syncopation. It was like forty shooting stars firing off at once, each one exploding again and again and together, they were as bright as a galaxy. We whooped and laughed, jumping higher and higher, like we were on the moon, like if we jumped high enough we could leave the ground and fly around.

But the Zodka began to weigh us down and finally we couldn't whoop no more. So we ducked back out through the hole in the fence, sneaked back through the old playground and crawled up into the pricker bushes on Pájaro Ridge. We found a spot in the dirt without snakes and hid out there, watching the whole valley light up like a fireworks show. *Click click click.*

Johnny passed his flask till we saw some red lights blinking over the hill, and knew the sheriff had arrived. We watched him drive up and get out of his car. He didn't blow his top or shout or nothing. He wasn't shocked or amazed. He walked around, scratching his half-gray beard.

We held our breath and tried not to giggle, while he looked around for whoever had started this trouble. Then we heard him sigh real heavy. He climbed onto the first school bus so slow, it was like he was fighting stronger gravity than we could feel, and he shut the first set of lights off.

Then he climbed back out, looked around at all the other lights, and sighed again.

As soon as he hoisted his tired self onto the second bus, Johnny bolted back through the hole in the fence. Like a maniac, he slid down the hill toward the sheriff, scattering a cloud of dust and twigs.

"Johnny!" I hissed.

He ducked behind the sheriff's car and waited there where we could see him and the sheriff couldn't. The second set of lights turned off, and the sheriff climbed down from the second bus.

Me and Ray and Eduardo watched in silence, strung out on a new feeling. On the thrill of danger.

Johnny opened the sheriff's passenger-side door and ducked inside. What was he doing? This was not part of my idea. It was some crazy, next-dimension expansion I had never imagined.

One by one, the sheriff climbed onto each bus, shut off the lights, and climbed down again. That magical glow of lights began to fade.

Johnny rolled out of the car onto the ground. He jumped up, slammed the door and booked to the hole in the fence. The sheriff continued his rounds — didn't even notice Johnny.

When the last golden light switched off, and there was only the rhythmic red pulse of the sheriff's lights in the dark, Johnny darted back up the hill, and crashed in the dirt between us.

"Why did you do that?" I whispered. "He almost saw you!"

"I know!" Johnny laughed, catching his breath. Then he stared at me a second and his expression changed. He shrugged, and held up a brand new, unopened pack of smokesticks. He'd taken it from the car.

"All that for smokes?"

"No, dummy. It's not about—" He sighed, like I was a dumb little kid. "He left 'em right on the seat, and now they're mine." And he cracked the pack open. "Jeez."

Johnny popped the business end of a fresh smokestick in his mouth, and we all sat there in silence, listening to him chew. For a long minute, it seemed like nothing would ever break that spell.

Down below, the sheriff leaned against the car.

At last, Johnny made a kind of disdainful snort. He shoved the smokestick back in the box, and sat up real straight. "I'm outta here."

"Where we off to next, Johnny?" Eduardo asked quickly.

But Johnny was looking away, down the valley. "Nah. I guess I've wasted enough time here with you losers."

Ray and Eduardo said nothing, and I didn't either. I felt sick. Sad, all of a sudden, like I'd been kicked in the gut.

I had let Johnny down. I'd done my best but those lights weren't enough. I remembered all those school bus lights winking like fireflies trapped in a jar, and I recalled the joy I'd felt sitting here and watching them. What a loser. I felt my face turn red.

The sheriff got into his parked car and filled out paperwork. One foot in the gravel, the other on the gas, while his red lights flashed.

"On to bigger and better things." Johnny rose to his feet. "Life's too short."

And he walked away through the dust.

There was something final about it. At that moment I knew that come Monday morning, Johnny wouldn't be in school. I felt my heart would break. I wanted to call out to him. Johnny was the most exciting thing that had ever happened in Albedo. If we couldn't keep him, then we wouldn't be able to keep nothing great. And there was no hope for this place, nor any future in it neither.

But me and Ray and Eduardo sat there and watched him go. We finished the rest of Johnny's flask without a word. When I stood up at last, the world was spinning hard.

"That was cool though," said Eduardo, looking hopefully at me from the dirt. "Right, Glen?"

I turned my back and left them there. I didn't look around, even when Ray said "Hey Glen! Where you goin', Glen?"

I kept on walking. I didn't want those two losers to follow me around no more.

That night, I couldn't sleep. On the highway, traffic was heavy. Some nights are like that. Cars roared past. Hovertrucks rattled my windowpanes. A fat fly bumped against the screen, trying to get out, and I lay there with the whiskey sweats, tangled up in my sheets, watching the room spin.

I thought I heard Johnny's beat up Pontiac. I imagined it idling at the on-ramp, waiting for a break in traffic. I sprung out of bed but my foot was all twisted in the sheets and I fell to the floor. I peeled off the sheets, pulled on sweatpants, and bolted outside into the night.

"Hey Johnny, can I come with you?" I was still a little drunk.

A hovertruck thundered by. My hair blew back from my face, and the deep bass hit me like a blow. I could have reached out and touched it.

A pair of taillights pulled up to the on-ramp. A Pontiac. I ran after it, shouting, but that car pulled out, merged into the river of traffic and washed away. And anyway, it was us losers Johnny had to get away from.

So I went and got my old hunting rifle, and I lay down in the grass. The rifle felt good in my grip, cold and solid. I watched more cars go by. Everybody had some place to go. And I didn't have anything in mind. I was aimless.

But with that rifle in my hands, I had the power to make some difference, if I chose to.

I pointed it across the highway, and peered through my scope, clear into the desert. I could see a field of stupid, misshapen saguaros over there, all lit up by the moon. A whole bunch of dumb cactus trees, with their arms and legs akimbo like they were dancing.

I used to try shooting one of those cactus arms off. I don't know why. It was hard to hit one, and I didn't have nothing against them, but it felt good, seeing something happen, and knowing I caused it.

Through the scope tonight, the headlights were a blur. The traffic was not a wall, anymore, not a barrier, but something like water that you might be able to pass through. No harder than crossing a river.

I was squinting through the scope when I saw something dark move on *this* side of the road. I lowered the rifle and there he was — a big daddy jackrabbit, sitting in the shadow of a stone. He was looking across the highway like he was gonna make a run for it.

"Don't do it," I said. "Too many cars tonight." I raised the hunting rifle again, spotting a saguaro through the scope.

That jackrabbit sat there, waiting. Watching the waves of cars go by.

"Go back down your hole!" I said. "This ain't your night."

I lowered the gun, annoyed. He was coiled like a mousetrap, ready to spring. If I shot my gun, the sound would startle him, and he'd dash straight into that river of lights and hissing tires and screaming metal grills.

"Stupid jackrabbit. Shoo."

The ground shook with the deep thunder of a howertruck.

But he didn't move. He was ready to make a dash for it and if that was what he was gonna do, that was what he was gonna do.

So I brought up my rifle, aimed at one of the dancing saguaros, and on the first try I clean shot its arm off.

The crack resounded over the highway. That jackrabbit bolted straight into the oncoming traffic.

He didn't stand a chance. So without really thinking, I stepped up onto the shoulder. "Watch out!"

I was on my feet at the edge of the highway, me and my hunting rifle, wearing no shirt, just my sweatpants and my whiskey sweat.

With a roar, the first truck swerved to miss me, and rumbled on past. I didn't pay it no attention. I could still see the jackrabbit, halfway across the asphalt. He was frozen in place in the stream of oncoming lights. Crouched down, between the second and third lane, like he was staring down an eagle or snake.

Another truck sped toward him. So without giving it too much thought, I stepped over the white line and waved my arms at him.

"Go, little guy!"

The next truck swerved to miss me. But he didn't see the oldsmobile there.

Amidst the squeal of brakes, and the crush of twisted metal, and the diamond spray of smashing glass, and before the fire broke out and the yelling started, I saw his mad dash. That big daddy jackrabbit set his eyes on the other side, and he went for it. Through the chaos and clear into to the field.

After that night, they put me on probation. And somewhere along the line, it was like a light went out for me and Ray and Eduardo. We didn't have anything to do with each other, anymore.

Every kid has friends and big ideas. Maybe some have good friends, like Ray and Eduardo. Maybe some even make a notebook like mine. But I don't guess anyone has that when they get older. You got to make a break from all that some time. You got to concern yourself with other things. Finding someplace to live. Keeping fed.

I heard Eduardo married a girl from down San Vincente somewheres, and they have kids on the way. Your friends and adventures were just a thing of the moment, I guess.

Not something to keep.

<hr>

THE ISLAND IS quiet except for the waves lapping at the rocky shore. Hard to imagine it's full of guards with guns.

I look down at my feet, planted on dry land. In the darkness at the water's edge, sea foam is piling up like shaving cream. Eerie in the starlight. Maybe this is normal, where you have so much water. I don't know, I never saw the ocean before yesterday.

"Now when I say *go*," says Johnny, "you head that way, towards them lights." I see the faint amber glow of a guard outpost over the ridge. "Crab your way over them rocks."

The foam is caked on my pants. I wipe my hands on my shirt while I look around at a bunch of desolate boulders and ruin.

I want to trust Johnny. I *know* he's up to something — I ain't stupid. But that doesn't mean he's not looking out for me. He's not telling me everything, but he still has my back. Both things can be true.

My ears perk up. There's a sound like a motor running. Soft idling, like snoring, out in the dark.

"You hear that?" I say.

"No," says Johnny. "Nope."

I look out at the bay. "Is there another boat out there?" I see nothing. But *would* you see? If there was another boat out there with its running lights shut dark, waiting?

"Hell no," says Johnny, rummaging in his black and red

duffel. "You'll be fine, Glen. You were born for this. Nobody *ever* notices you!"

I know the plan. But now I really need to hear Johnny say it. I need him to tell me what he's gonna do, and how it'll be all right. I need to know that after all this time we've been apart, and even though he's changed, somehow, he's still like a big brother to me.

"And you'll bring the boat around, right?" I say. My voice sounds weak, almost desperate. "And meet me on the other side? That's the plan?"

Johnny fidgets with his phone.

"Right?" I push. "When it's all over?"

Johnny's body tenses all up and for an instant he looks at me like a hawk at a field mouse. "Glen." He cocks an eyebrow. "Are you really gonna ask me that?"

And the eels are back, slithering up my throat. I hunch over a little, holding my gut. Everything's all wrong. I knew it.

"Four minutes," says Johnny, punching my arm. "Go!"

All fours, I crab up over the rocks, not thinking, just making for the top of the ridge as fast as I can in the dark. I had believed an island might be squishy, like a mud patty, surrounded by all that water, but the ground here is hard. These rocks are sharper than the ones back home. Jagged and rough.

When I reach the top of the ridge, I duck real low to keep beneath the motion sensor's line of sight. I crawl along the ridge-line, like a worm. I do not wanna see that silver kill light come on.

From the shore, I feel Johnny's eyes on me. Craning my neck around, I see him gesturing in the dark. He holds up four fingers. *Four minutes.* I know!

Are the motion sensors off? Or am I dead? I never been so scared. My palms sweat. My heart beats something wild, and I raise my head to peak over the horizon.

No kill light.

They're off. Like Johnny said they would be.

Here's one thing. If he doesn't meet me on the other side, if he doesn't come around with the boat like he promised, how will he get the dreamcatcher? He can't. He can't get that if he doesn't meet me. Right? So whatever's his plan, I know that at least. So don't panic then. Just do my part and trust Johnny to take care of the rest.

Over the other side, I see the guard's outpost, maybe twenty yards down the slope. It's lit by a glow from a screen inside. And beyond that, another ridge and past that, I see the black tower itself, rising like a knobby hunchback against the fog. It looks small from here. What kind of fortress would the prawn king build for himself?

Crap. I forgot to set the stopwatch! I pull myself up to elbow height in the shelter of a big, friendly boulder. I fiddle with the buttons and the black screen starts blinking green.

3:59. 3:58. 3:57.

But that's not real. I must have lost ten seconds before I remembered the watch.

I peer down at the outpost below. Sure enough, there's a guard in there. The replacement guard should already be coming down from the tower for the shift change, but I don't see him. Where is he?

I turn back and shoot Johnny a questioning look. He gives me a thumbs-up.

Behind him, something catches my eye. Coming out of the water on the left — a black hoverboat. It's crawling with guys. They're dressed in black, bristling with blades and gas masks. What are we breathing? I catch the glint of starlight on gunmetal. I rub my eyes and stare.

Ninjas?

Johnny spots them too. Without fuss, he throws the hoverboat into reverse. Keeping his face low to the console, he backs away from shore. He doesn't look at me or nothing.

He just fades away.

The ninjas steer their silent hoverboat right up among the rocks and pile out.

I lie low and still on the rocks behind my big friendly boulder, while they storm up the ridge toward me. No one stays back to guard their boat. I worm in closer behind the boulder and hold my breath. Now what?

They suspect nothing. Fear no one. They don't notice me. They charge past me and my boulder. I feel the ground shake beneath their boots. I smell engine grease and leather and I lie here hoping they don't look down.

And then they've over the ridge and rushing downhill, and I can hear them swarming the guard post. The replacement guard is finally on his way from the tower. He looks up and shouts something. With a sudden crack like thunder they start shooting guns at him. It's so loud I can't even think. *One. Two-three. Four-five-six.*

The replacement guard cries out once, and then I can't see him no more through the ninjas, and the shooting stops.

Inside the post, the screen goes out. The darkness and silence is worse than shooting. Or is it? I wish I never came. My head is ringing.

There comes a burst of machine gun fire from the guard post. One of the ninjas goes down. The booth guard got him!

They didn't expect that. The booth guard, who was supposed to be getting off work, has decided to defend his post. It's stupid and hopeless but maybe he's more afraid of his boss than the invaders. A dumb guard caught between Molek the prawn king and a team of killer ninjas.

He sprays another bunch of bullets wildly across the rocks

and then one of the ninjas walks up behind him and fires a shot into the booth.

The ninjas regroup in businesslike silence and continue on their way up to the tower. They leave behind two dead guards — and one of their own fallen. If they've come for the dreamcatcher, a few dead bodies are not gonna slow them down.

Whoever they work for must be as scary as the prawn king.

I got to gather my thoughts. My ears are ringing. The air tastes like metal. How much time is left? My hand shakes so hard I can barely read the glowing green numbers on my stopwatch. They're blurring and jittering, bouncing up and down, as I try to hold steady and now I see and I can barely believe what it says:

1:08. 1:07. 1:06

What have I done? This was the biggest distraction ever possible. A ninja attack! This was all maybe in Johnny's plan! The part he didn't tell me about. I should have used this time to keep crawling, like Johnny said, all the way up to the tower, and then worm my way in, grab the dreamcatcher, and get back to the boat. Those ninjas would never have noticed me in all the commotion. But instead I froze up and now I don't know what to do. What *can* you do?

What if I'm still behind this rock when the timer hits zero and the motion sensors come back on? What if those invaders get the dreamcatcher, and start using it to distort reality, and the land folds itself, or the sky opens up, or what have you? Or time freezes or stretches? What would guys like that do with such reality distorting power? They could turn the land to sea, or start fires that will never burn out. They could go full-on nightmare time, with spiders or T-rex or ghouls.

The fallen ninja is moving.

Crawling.

His leg is dragging, but he's pulling himself slowly up the slope toward me. I hear him grunt. He looks at his wristwatch.

It's green like mine, and he doesn't like what he sees on the screen. He's exposed in the rockfield. He crawls faster.

He's fixing to hide behind *my* boulder before time runs out. Does he realize *I'm* here?

I glance back at the shore. In the tall grass, the ninja boat stands empty, bobbing up and down in the waves. Other than that it's just darkness and nothing. I'm on my own.

The ninja pulls himself along the ground. He's looking right at me. He knows I'm here. He knows I'm not armed. I'm not a threat. There's no room behind this boulder for two of us, there just isn't. He's gonna take me out.

My heart is pounding. He's gonna take my place before the timer counts down, then wait behind my boulder for his buddies to come back through with the all powerful dreamcatcher and rescue him.

There's a flash of ghostly tungsten light — a bolt of lightning so cold and so bright that for an instant it sucks all the color from the world and reveals the true nature of everything — black and white. Black tower looming against white fog. Black ninja crawling against white rocks. The kill light.

Our whole zone is lit up like the moon. There's a shady area down around the curve of the hill — the next zone I guess — but there's no way to get to it. Our motion sensors have triggered and, here in this zone, it's high noon.

The crawling ninja knows the rules have changed. He freezes cold.

I check my body against the stone. All black. All shadow. I'm hidden. I pull my hands and feet in closer behind my boulder to be sure.

My watch is still counting down from 0:15 when I hear the sentinels skittering towards us.

They clamber over the rocks like scorpions — military land

drones. Their skin shimmers like liquid silver, and their eyes shine with pixels.

They skitter across the floodlit rocks and pool like oil around the fallen ninja. He's hidden his face in the crook of his arm, and now he lies perfectly still. A pile of rags. Maybe he's as scared as a little boy, half-woke from a nightmare, who wishes he could call for his mother.

The scorpions swarm him. Their stingers flash. They're agitated, they vibrate, but they don't touch him. Not yet. Maybe they're waiting to be sure. Or maybe listening for something. Or enjoying the moment.

I'm shaking again but I force myself still. No movement at all. I try to hold my breath.

A tiny, wicked little sentinel, the leader maybe, lowers its tail over him, like a pregnant wasp, and it waits. The ninja holds his breath. Stills his heart. Maybe he can fool them. He's trained for this.

I see the tower beyond the ridge behind them. I know what I have to do.

I gotta go. Make a break for it. Now.

I scramble to my feet and bolt out into the light. I run without thinking, on terror and instinct. Half-blinded in the glare of the kill lights, I tear across the rocky ground, running toward the sentinel swarm and the tower beyond. Hoping I can jump high enough.

These scorpions have their hands full. They're not looking at me. As I approach, the ninja looks up. He raises his arm, as if reaching for me.

I leap, high as I can, and sail clear over them all. The sentinels below are all murder and death. And now I crash down on the other side of 'em, feet thudding over the ground, and I *book*. Up the next ridge, toward the tower.

I can see it beyond the rockfield. I don't know what I'll do when I get there but now I can see the door at its base, blown open in battle, stained with smoke, I can make it, I know I can. I'm flying —

I look back over my shoulder. The lead sentinel's stinger stabs down. The ninja jolts like he's been connected to something. I hear him grunt through gritted teeth, and the littlest scorpion holds him there a minute, and then scuttles away. The ninja sighs softly, and then goes quiet.

He lies there, face down among the rocks and steams.

The scorpions look up again. Pixel eyes scanning the rocks again in the glare of the kill lights.

Instinctively I freeze.

It's an awkward position — like a runner about to cross the finish line. My right arm is raised over my head, reaching for the gold but not grasping it yet. My neck is twisted around to gawk — but the predator's eyes are on me, I can feel them looking. And I'm stuck again, in the shadow of the tower.

The wasp sentinel waggles its tail and the others fall in behind it, picking their way toward me across the rockfield.

I try not to breathe. My heart pounds. Standing in the kill light, my muscles already ache. My long shadow is thrown out before me, and I can see my pulse in its rhythmic trembling. So can they. They rattle toward me, faster now. Their mandibles clicking. Like a rush of oncoming traffic. Like a wave about to wash me away.

They're at my feet, and still I don't move. They sense, taste the air, deciding what to do. *I'm not a threat.* I don't move but I can feel my right arm fatiguing. *I'm not even here.* I wish I'd frozen in a more natural position. *I'm nothing.* Or stayed at my boulder. *If you look at me, you won't even see me.*

Above my head, my right arm begins to tremble.

I wish I'd never come to this island. I wish I was back washing dishes at the Hi-Spot. That I'd never followed Johnny out to that parking lot. That I'd never left Albedo. That rusted-out trailer was mine, after Pa left. I could still live by the side of the highway, among the jackrabbits and the dust and the stars.

The scorpions fall still. I've fooled them, for the moment. They're waiting like hunters, ready to kill the very next thing that moves in their world. How long can I hold my position?

A movement catches my eye in the distance — below the ridge line, in the next zone where it's dark, and the kill lights don't shine.

That's Johnny. He's coming down the back side of the hill. Walking along, as cocky as can be.

He's carrying a big black egg. It's the size of a bowling ball, with maybe twenty sides, and it's as black as the sky at night. I never seen anything so black. Johnny cradles it like the gift of the magi.

He's already got it.

He sees me surrounded by scorpions. Lit up in the kill lights. I don't dare move anything but my eyes, so I make eyes at him. I plead silently, willing him to hear me: *Don't leave me here, Johnny.*

Looking me right in the eye, he tosses that dreamcatcher in the air. Casual as a kid tossing a yo-yo. He's practically whistling. The precious thing tumbles up into space above him, and then yo-yos back down. He catches it without breaking eye contact. Putting on a show for me. He's practically whistling. Cocky.

Please, Johnny.

And he gives me that look. The old Johnny look that says there is a bright center to the universe, where anything is possible. And with a sudden surge of ice water into my veins, as cold as Johnny's smile, I finally understand that look.

It's a look that says he's special, and so it's his choices that matter. Johnny's ideas that rule the world. And nobody else matters at all.

I see the edges of his mouth curl into a smile. But I can't do nothing about it. I stand here, frozen in place, and wonder how this will all end, even as I look down at the scorpions and think: *it's already ended.*

Over my shoulder, the dead ninja steams among the rocks. My strength is giving out. But I hold my position and I watch. It's like an instinct, out of some deep place. My heart's beating fast, but as long as I hold, only my eyes can give me away.

And nobody's looking into my eyes. Nobody ever did notice me when Johnny was around.

He tosses the dreamcatcher in the air again. A little higher, this time. As careless as can be. Making a show of it as he nears the water's edge.

It tumbles up, and up, maybe a little higher than he intended, and Johnny's smile suddenly drops off his face. His mouth opens as if he's gonna cry out. The dreamcatcher spins up, and up — to where the motion sensor's invisible beam, coming over the top of the ridge, catches it.

In Johnny's zone, where all was dark, the kill light comes on.

The scorpions turn toward him. Their thoraxes make a horrible scraping sound on the rocks, and that makes Johnny flinch. He fumbles the dreamcatcher and it splashes down at the water's edge.

The scorpions take off in a scurry, leaving me behind in their rush toward Johnny. Silver mandibles snick and pop in the glare of the kill light.

"Johnny, freeze!" I shout.

But he bends down to grab the dreamcatcher. Before he can scoop it up, they're on him. Crawling up his legs. Swarming his arms. He raises his hands to bat them away from his face, but they're everywhere. He's like that cartoon bear who tried to rob the honeybee tree.

With a start, not thinking about nothing but just reacting, I bolt. I charge toward him in a mad dash.

"No Johnny!" I can save him.

But he howls, falling to the rocks as the scorpions raise their tails. I'm here with him now at the water's edge but too late. I can already hear the electric *snap* of their stingers against his skin.

So I pivot in a fluid motion, and spring right past him. Splash into the water. I scoop up the dreamcatcher with both hands. It weighs nothing, like a helium balloon at a birthday party. I catch my breath, and dry the dreamcatcher carefully on my shirt. Knee-deep in water, I look around.

Johnny isn't moving anymore. The sentinels are busy over him. There's rocks and swamp grass beneath my feet. Out among the reeds, half-hidden in the darkness beyond the kill lights, I see Johnny's hoverboat.

I slog deeper. Immersed, now, in the rush of water, I reach the boat.

I roll the dreamcatcher onto the deck, and hoist myself aboard after it.

Trembling on the deck, I look back. It's dark. All the kill lights have gone out. If there's any sound at all from the island, it's lost beneath the rush of waves and surf. Can sentinels swim?

I fiddle with the boat's navigation unit, typing in the only coordinates that I can remember. They come straight to mind, even though it's been a while. I think this other touchscreen adjusts the speed.

The engines whine to life, and pretty soon I'm flying across the water. I set the dreamcatcher, humming quietly to itself, on the vinyl seat.

Something catches my foot and almost trips me up. I glance down at Johnny's black and red duffel on the deck. Without thinking, I scoop it up and toss it overboard. It was near empty. I don't think there was ever a signal jammer in that bag. I look back one last time and see the island disappearing behind me.

Up ahead, the first glimmers of sunrise appear. By daylight, the water seems less scary. Its glittering surface is kind of beautiful, even. All this movement. Everything always shifting and changing. It doesn't feel like it's masking fearsome depths anymore. It feels like anything is possible.

I hold the dreamcatcher. It vibrates and buzzes against my fingertips. Powerful. Electric. Now that it's mine, I admit, I don't know what to do with a military grade dreamcatcher. Don't know how to use it, or even what the possibilities are. But I don't think I'm gonna go back to the Hi-Spot and wash dishes anymore.

Back home, under my bed in the old trailer, I got some ideas written down. A whole notebook full of them. The wind picks up. Maybe Ray and Eduardo will want to try a few.

PURPLE SOCK
LAURIE CALKHOVEN

When a socially invisible high school girl impulsively steals her neighbor's laundry, she ultimately brings down a bully and finally feels seen by her classmates.

Book coach and children's book author Laurie Calkhoven has published more than fifty books for children and teens ranging from early readers and funny chapter books to historical novels that bring the wacky facts of history to light. When she's not writing or reading, she can be found roaming around the museums, theaters, and parks of New York City. Visit her at https:// lauriecalkhoven.com

PLAYLIST

Girls Just Want To Have Fun — **Cyndi Lauper**
Like A Virgin — **Madonna**
What Difference Does It Make? — **The Smiths**

Scan to listen at buttonhall.com/books/left-turns

O kay, here's how it started. I'm not a real criminal. It was temporary insanity. One minute I was doing my homework; the next I was stealing.

I, Rebecca Jacobs, committed laundry thievery.

I had started a load of wash in the laundry room of my New York City apartment building and stayed to work on my French irregular verbs—the laundry room being the only place where my little brother was guaranteed not to bug me. I was sitting there trying to remember the difference between *devoir* and *vouloir*, cursing the fact that I had left *Discover Le Français* (or was it *La Française)* upstairs, and breathing in competing detergent scents when I saw Ainsley Abbott's purple sock going around and around in the dryer.

I knew it was Ainsley's because her mom was putting her wet laundry into the dryer when I walked in with my dirty clothes.

Mrs. Abbott was way friendlier than her daughter. "Hey, Rebecca," she said. "Are you excited about the school dance on Friday?"

I grunted something that she must have taken for a yes.

"Ainsley and her friends have been planning what to wear for days."

"Well, she always looks nice," I mumbled. Really what I was thinking was that they would all look like Madonna wannabes, but whatever. I once mentioned the Smiths to one of the Issas— it was hard to tell them apart—and she stared at me like I had two heads. Cyndi Lauper was about as far as Ainsley was willing to go into alternative music, and her followers didn't dare be different.

Ainsley's mom left the laundry room, and I went back to my French verbs—at least until I saw a purple sock tumbling by through the dryer's glass door.

Ainsley had big plans for that sock. Earlier that day I was hanging out in my usual lunchtime spot—a bathroom stall—re-

reading *The Chocolate Wars* and making a list of ways my high school was like Trinity High—when she and her ladies-in-waiting came in to admire themselves.

"Wear purple socks tomorrow," Ainsley had said.

Melissa, Clarissa, and Alissa (otherwise known as the Issas) cooed, "Oooooh, that's so cool, Ainsley. No one else will be wearing purple socks."

Like wearing socks of any color was a major accomplishment.

There's not much we can do to our uniforms at Kimberley Girls' Academy, but this was "Wacky Week." We were supposed to get wackier with our uniforms every day up until "Freaky Friday" when we got to wear our own clothes and have a dance with the ninth-grade boys from the Pingrey Boys' School—hence the "Like a Virgin" clones who would be filling the auditorium on Friday. And yes, it was 1985, but our schools were stuck in the 1950s.

It was *mandatory* dance, so even a six-foot tall gawk with a huge red zit on the tip of her nose had to go.

Today, the Issas were wearing red bow ties instead of the Kimberley Academy uniform tie. Ainsley, of course, had to stand out. Hers had sparkles.

There was extended cooing about the purple socks until one of Ainsley's followers said something about how all the boys from Pingrey would be falling for her precious highness.

"Like I'm going to dance with a freshman," Ainsley answered.

I had a clear view of her sneer through the crack in the bathroom stall door.

She stopped applying her lip gloss and eyeballed each one of the Issas for emphasis. "None of you should dance with underclassmen. We're too mature. If there were going to be juniors and seniors there, then maybe. But we aren't dancing with any ninth graders."

"We aren't going to dance at all?"

I think it was Melissa who asked.

"With the children? I don't think so," Ainsley declared. Her tone made Melissa shrink back as if she had been slapped.

"But I like to dance," Clarissa whined.

"Dance all you want with the little boys. The grownups will be otherwise engaged," Ainsley said.

Clarissa darted her gaze back and forth from Melissa to Alissa, but they were quiet.

Finally, Alissa broke the tension with an age-old ploy to make Ainsley laugh—making fun of me.

"Hey, who do you think will dance with your neighbor—the tall one with the nose?"

Ainsley snorted. "They'll come up to her boobs. Oh wait, I forgot, she doesn't have any."

My face burned. I *was* tall and skinny and flat-chested. I knew Ainsley had it in for me, but what had I done to the rest of them?

Then Ainsley reminded them about the purple socks. "Don't tell anyone. I don't want any of these geeks copying us."

And now, just a few hours later, there was a fluffy, purple sock tumbling dry right in front of me.

What if . . .

No. I won't stoop to her stupid level. Who cares about socks?

But then the thought crossed my mind again. *What if . . .*

Under the glare of the laundry room's fluorescent lights, I hatched a plan.

There were three minutes left on the dryer's timer. Mrs. Abbott was one of those people who showed up the minute her laundry was finished—not like Mr. Campbell in 4B whose laundry could sit in the dryer for days before he made his way back downstairs.

If I was going to do this, I had to act fast.

I ran to the door and peeked into the hallway. No one was around.

Two minutes left on the timer.

I opened the dryer door, letting the hot air hit my face while I waited for the clothes to stop swirling around.

One minute left on the timer.

It has to be now.

Something wrapped itself around my arm. I burned my fingers on a zipper. Then there it was! A purple sock. I grabbed it and slammed the dryer shut just as the elevator doors dinged open.

I shoved the sock and whatever else had wrapped itself around my arm into my backpack and shoved it under the table. I had to sit on my hands so that Ainsley's mom wouldn't see them trembling.

I was breathing so hard I was sure she could hear me gasping all the way from the elevator.

What if she folds everything in front of me and sees that a sock is missing? Will she ask me if I saw it?

An electric flash ran through my body as I imagined her catching me in a lie. Demanding that I empty my backpack in front of her, marching me upstairs like a five-year-old to humiliate me by forcing me to hand over Ainsley's sock with an apology. I could almost see the posters with my yearbook picture hanging in the laundry room with the message: BEWARE. LAUNDRY THIEF.

But Mrs. Abbot dumped her dried laundry into a basket, and with a "Have a nice night," breezed into the hall and back onto the elevator.

My clothes were halfway through their own dryer cycle before my heart settled down to a normal pace.

It wasn't until I got upstairs and closed myself in my bedroom that I examined the evidence of my thievery: one purple sock, a pink tee shirt, and a bra (padded, hah!) with Ainsley's name written on the label in permanent marker. I guess it was one she brought to summer camp.

When I could, I'd destroy the evidence by sending it down the building's garbage chute, but right now I merely stashed it in the back of my closet, behind the stack of *Nancy Drew* novels I haven't been able to bring myself to give away.

I expected to have trouble sleeping that night—I had become a thief after all—but I conked right out and slept until the alarm rang the next morning.

I was getting ready for school when I heard the purple sock commotion. Ainsley was yelling loud enough for me to hear right through the bedroom wall we share. The words were muffled, but her tone of outrage came through loud and clear. *Hah!*

That morning she stood at the bus stop with a look that would compel any mother to warn her that her face would get stuck like that if she didn't stop. I glanced at her socks—regulation navy blue.

"What are you looking at, freak?" she snapped.

I looked away so she wouldn't see me smile.

My feud with Ainsley, or rather her feud with me, started when I moved into the building eight years ago. My mother was so excited to find a girl my age living right next door that she not only enrolled me in the same private girls' school but bought me a Strawberry Shortcake backpack and lunch box just like Ainsley's. I thought it would make us best friends, but on the first day of school Ainsley scribbled all over Strawberry and Lemon Meringue with permanent black marker. On the second, she tripped me on the playground. On the third, I carried a new

Jetsons backpack, but the damage had been done. Ainsley's small world had been crushed by the horror of carrying the same backpack as me. I had been doing my best to be invisible ever since, and I was mostly successful. Every once in a while our mothers tried to force us to do something together, and I'd find myself on the receiving end of Ainsley's wrath for the next few weeks.

Ainsley had always been classically pretty—long blonde hair, big blue eyes. She didn't go through that horrible awkward phase that overtook most of us in the beginning of sixth grade. I don't think she ever even had a zit.

My own awkward phase started when I shot up three inches in the summer between fifth and sixth grades, and it had yet to end. I was convinced now that it never would. The more awkward I got, the meaner Ainsley became.

She was smart, too, so teachers loved her. And brilliant enough to hide her mean streak from parents and principals and teachers.

Most of the freshman class had been on the receiving end of Ainsley's withering attention at one point or another. We all came up through the ranks of the lower school into ninth grade. But I was one of her favorite targets, and more than one kid in our school had gained Ainsley's approval by joining in.

The best I could hope for in making it through our all-girls' high school was to be as obscure as possible so as not to make myself a target. Invisible was a comfortable place for me to be.

If Ainsley ever found out that I was the reason for her sock debacle, then I'd have to quit school and join the witness protection program.

By second period on purple sock day, the Issas had removed theirs in solidarity, and I thought my crime had been committed for nothing more than a few Issa blisters.

Or had it? In my fifth period elective—anthropology—we were creating a display in the main hallway's glass case about ancient body adornment. I was hanging a picture of an Egyptian chick with an elaborate necklace and a bizarre wax thing on her head when insanity struck a second time.

Which is when I went from a normal kid who had committed one small laundry crime to a criminal mastermind.

The bell rang, and I offered to return the supplies to the classroom. Doddering old Mrs. Bernays said thanks and hobbled off to the teacher's lounge. The key she had given me to the glass display case "slipped" into my pocket instead of making it back to her classroom.

The next morning, I told my mother I had to be at school early and carefully packed my backpack.

I kept my head down and hoped my uniform and regular anonymity would keep me invisible. Still, kamikaze butterflies did dive bombs in my stomach as girls wandered in for pre-school clubs or for whatever bizarre reasons girls came to school earlier than they absolutely had to.

By 7:30 there was a new exhibit in the middle of the ancient Greeks and Egyptians.

Ainsley's bra was the centerpiece. Over it, I had pinned a sign I printed out the night before that read:

MODERN COURTING RITUALS.

Some of today's girls, at least ones without redeeming personality features, need more than jewelry and makeup to attract mates. Thus, the padded bra was born. Used to give an illusion of actual breasts, it is primarily worn by insecure teenage girls.

Bra provided courtesy of Ainsley Abbott

I hid around the corner and waited. I watched girls saunter, step, stroll, and stride into the main hall, depending on the distance/time ratio from locker to homeroom. No one noticed the bright, white bra in the middle of the Egyptian display.

Was all that for nothing? I wondered.

Finally, a junior did a double take. She stopped to read and giggled. A small crowd gathered. Soon the laughs were loud and extended.

Most of the school moved on. But the ninth-grade girls waited to see what Ainsley would do. We all lived in fear of her ability to turn even a popular girl into one of the untouchables in a matter of seconds. *Can that change?*

By the time Ainsley strutted through the entrance doors into the main hallway—Issas trailing behind her in matching aqua tee shirts and headbands—half of the Kimberley Girls' Academy had seen her padded bra on display.

Ainsley took in the small crowd. "What's this," she said to the Issas, "a geek fest?"

They laughed, on cue.

The other girls parted, leaving a clear path between Ainsley and the display case. Some of my fellow students looked the way my cat did when a bird flew too close to the window.

Ainsley walked toward the display case with a smirk. Her tone was sarcastic when she started to read. "Some of today's girls, especially ones without redeeming personality features, need more than jewelry and makeup to attract mates." She stopped and looked around.

Michelle Gilbert, pretty but slightly overweight, was the first girl to catch Ainsley's eye.

"Would that be you, Michelle?" Ainsley asked, her voice filled with elaborate sweetness.

Instead of slinking away, Michelle raised her chin a little.

Ainsley's voice got louder in response to the Issas' laughter. It's a good thing I tower over the entire freshman class, or I wouldn't have been able to see her face when she came to the last line.

"Bra provided courtesy of...." Her face turned red, then white, then red again.

Issa jaws dropped.

I held my breath.

The first bell rang; no one moved.

Ainsley screamed. "Who did this?" She glared at the faces around her. Her eyes went right past me.

I almost sighed at my good fortune. My invisibility held.

"Which one of you jealous little witches did this?"

Silence.

Ainsley stamped her foot. "That's not my bra."

I heard a giggle, then a snort as the crowd tried not to laugh and then gave up and let go.

"I'm calling my mother!" Ainsley screamed.

Girls held on to their stomachs, the wall, and each other in one great big belly laugh while Ainsley screamed "Get it down! Get it down!"

Clarissa suppressed a giggle as she and the other Issas tried to help Ainsley open the cabinet. It was locked, and I had thrown away the key.

Melissa tried to give Ainsley a hug, but Ainsley pushed her away. "Get the janitor!" she squawked. "Get the principal."

The principal stopped short when she was close enough to see the bra. She tried to read the explanation, but Ainsley was screeching in her ear.

"I want that out of there. NOW! Then I want you to find out who did this to me, and I want them expelled. EXPELLED!"

The principal tried to calm her.

"If that's not out of there in 30 seconds, I'll sue. My father's a lawyer!"

Melissa came back with the janitor. When old Mr. Lamott

looked at Ainsley's bra and shook his head, even the Issas lost it. Clarissa sank to the floor, laughing hard enough to wet her pants.

Ainsley stood sputtering—too angry to make words—while the principal sent us all to class.

Seeing Ainsley angry and embarrassed for a few minutes was enough. It was time to end my reckless crime spree before I got caught. Then something weird happened.

In chem lab, Lisa Bloomfield refused to change her seat so that Ainsley wouldn't have to look at her "hideous" orange scarf, and at lunch Emily Kim didn't put the last Dove Bar back and take an ice cream sandwich when Ainsley announced she wanted a Dove Bar.

The weirdness continued.

In fifth period P.E., Ainsley's pointed remarks about personal space and a geek-free zone in the locker room were ignored. It became even clearer that the padded bra on display that morning was hers.

Throughout it all, I was getting whispered cheers, pats on the back, and high fives from girls I thought didn't know my name. Someone had obviously seen me at work in the lobby. I only hoped that Ainsley wouldn't hear about it.

I spent Thursday night trying on clothes. I expected to spend the entire dance in the bathroom reading *Of Mice and Men* for English class, but I didn't want to wear something awful, especially now that people noticed my existence.

Nothing I tried on looked right. I asked my mother to write a note saying that my family had joined a cult that forbade dancing and the wearing of non-uniform clothes. She refused.

I spent extra time on my hair Friday morning, but it looked the way it always does—mousey brown and stick straight. I thought about putting on make-up, but why bother? At least the shining, red pimple on the tip of my nose had settled down into a less angry color.

I pulled on black jeans and an oversized sweater—not as anonymous as my uniform, but close. If it weren't for my height and my nose, I would go totally unnoticed.

I could hear Ainsley chattering on the phone next door the whole time I was getting ready. I couldn't make out words, but I could hear her voice rising and falling. No doubt planning some kind of revenge on the freshman class. Then I heard her laugh.

And I lost it.

I reached into the back of my closet and pulled out the stolen pink tee. I hadn't worn pink since the days my mother dressed me. It was tighter than anything I usually wore, but it fit.

Then I slipped into black tights and the black mini skirt my mother had insisted I buy for imaginary parties. Even I could see that I didn't look bad. If you were related to me, you might even say I looked good. At least I wouldn't humiliate myself on the way from the gym to the bathroom.

At the bus stop I felt as if Ainsley would be able to see her tee shirt right through my jacket, but all she did was look at my legs and turn away.

Her position at the top had almost been restored, but I still heard the occasional, "Way to go, Rebecca," and even, "Hey, great outfit."

It was lunchtime before I saw Ainsley again. Michelle had asked me why I was always disappearing at lunch time, so I braved the cafeteria with her. My invisibility shield was wobbling, and that felt okay.

Ainsley kept narrowing her eyes at me from across the sea of bad pizza as if trying to remember who I was.

I managed to avoid her after that, but there was no way to hide after school. Instead of going back to homeroom, we had to go to the gym, where we got a lecture on being charming host-esses while we waited for the boys. I hoped that the boys had gotten a similar lecture about not being jerks, but our school barely acknowledged that the 1950s had come and gone, let alone the 60s and the 70s.

The boys slouched in and stood on one side of the gym while we—a sea of Madonna look alikes, a few daring Cyndi Laupers, and me—stood on the other. Only one of the boys was taller than me, and just as skinny. He had red hair and big ears.

Jennifer McCutcheon, class president, asked a boy to dance. His friends laughed, but he said yes. The student council followed her lead. The rest of us watched them make fools out of themselves in the center of the gym.

That's the moment when the fact that was buzzing around in the back of Ainsley's brain since lunch must have flown to the front of her mind. If we were cartoon characters, a light bulb would have blinked on over her head.

She stopped making fun of the dancers and whispered to the Issas. The four of them pushed Michelle Plotnick out of the way and marched in my direction.

I tried to edge my way out of the gym, but I wasn't fast enough.

"That's a nice shirt," Ainsley smiled. "I'd love to get one just like it. Where did you buy yours?"

"I don't remember."

"You must like it a lot." She smiled again. Issas tittered. "Like it enough to *steal*." She had raised her voice for the word steal and paused to let it reverberate. "Is it the shirt you wanted, or do you wish you could be me?"

People gathered, sensing tension.

My invisibility shield wasn't wobbling. It was gone. "Excuse me." I tried to move around her. The Issas blocked my exit.

I heard the words "fight, fight," muttered in a sweaty, male voice.

"I always knew you were a freak, but I never guessed that you hung around the laundry room to steal my clothes."

I stood mute.

"You took my tee shirt from the laundry room, and you were the one who hung my . . . you were the one who made that sign about me."

"I feel sorry for you," Melissa chimed in. "You must be mentally ill."

My heart was hammering. I thought about what *The Chocolate Wars'* Jerry Renault would do. I stretched my body up to its full height, put on an Ainsley face, and lied.

"I don't think this shirt would fit you." I looked pointedly at the tight shirt she was wearing, a snug fit over her padded bra. "But if you really like it, I could give it to you."

One of the boys snorted and started muttering, "Take it off. Take it off" He was wearing enough cologne to choke half the gym.

Thank goodness, no one joined him in his chant.

Ainsley shook her mane like a lion ready to pounce.

"I'll have you kicked out of this school. You were the one, admit it!"

I stared her down.

"Say I did it if that will make you happy," I said, achieving a level of bravado I didn't think possible. "With the way you leave your clothes lying around in the locker room, it could have been anyone. But if it will make you happy, Ainsley," I gave her a sweet smile, "go ahead and say I did it."

That's when the world tilted on its axis.

"No, I did it." Michelle Plotnick moved to stand next to me.

"I did it." Amanda Browne took my other side.

Soon a sea of voices—male and female—shouted, "I did it! I did it!"

Alissa and Clarissa edged toward my side of the crowd. Melissa tried to follow, but Ainsley pulled her back.

Now Ainsley was the speechless one.

When the principal came to shoo us all onto the dance floor, Ainsley and Melissa stood alone.

Suddenly, the tall boy was next to me.

"What's with her?" he asked.

I shrugged.

"What a freak," he said.

I thought he meant me. Then I saw his eyes were on Ainsley. I bit my tongue so I wouldn't gasp.

"Hey, they're playing the Smiths! Wanna dance?" he asked.

I can imagine what we looked like from the outside. Two towering giants in the middle of the dance floor, all flailing arms and legs. Small people would be trampled in our midst.

And you know what?

I didn't care.

THE SPRING GROVE EXPERIMENT

REGINA SOKAS

Looking to escape a boring summer, a sixteen-year-old girl takes a job on a locked men's ward of the local state psychiatric hospital and learns more about life than she anticipated.

Regina Sokas has published straight-news, feature articles, poetry, and short stories. Her advertising copy was quoted on the front page of The Wall Street Journal. She has two completed novels currently in search of a home.

PLAYLIST

Eve of Destruction — **Barry McGuire**
Lay Lady Lay — **Bob Dylan**
Time of the Season — **The Zombies**
Flowers Never Bend in the Rainfall — **Simon and Garfunkle**
AQUARIUS — **The Fifth Dimension**

Scan to listen at buttonhall.com/books/left-turns

Most of my classmates didn't understand why I was spending my summer on one of the locked men's wards of the local state psychiatric hospital. Why had I actually volunteered to do this job, and for a little 'stipend,' a word that adults apparently invented so that they could feel good about paying you less than a third of minimum wage?

"You're not a man!" Laughter. That had been pretty obvious for a couple of years, since puberty hit me with the big end of the stick. "You're not crazy. Or are you?" I didn't really mind the teasing. At sixteen, this is as close to an adventure as I was going to get for my summer vacation. Babysitting? Waiting tables? Visiting my mother's family in Ohio? None of those things made my heart race a little faster. The hospital did.

This was the last week of the experiment. Not a drug experiment, although they were doing LSD experiments right there on the other side of the hospital campus. Turn on, tune in, drop out. That was Timothy Leary, and he was like the guru of acid trips, but he was Harvard. I heard they got away with a lot of weird shit up there.

No, I was part of a much more boring educational experiment. Somebody somewhere posed the question "What might happen if we gave high school students a two-day crash course in psychiatry and then scattered them in psychiatric hospitals around the state?"

My psych teacher made it sound like kind of a big deal idea. My photograph appeared in <u>The Catonsville Times</u> alongside a brief article announcing the program. I cut it out of the paper.

The first person I usually saw on the ward each morning was Little Old Italian Guy. He hovered in the small open hallway just outside the dayroom and the nurses' station, eyes flitting from one door to the other, scanning, scanning. Back always against the wall, so he never had to look behind him. I didn't know what his diagnosis was. That information was part of the sea of information that is never to be shared with the likes of me. Confidentiality did not include a kid like me.

Little Old Italian Guy was a small man. Shorter than me, and I was a pretty average five feet, four inches tall. Four and a half inches, on a good day. He always looked disheveled. Faded out. Like once upon a time he was technicolor, but then somebody washed him with bleach. He'd lost most of his hair, and the ones that remained appeared worried, on edge. Buzzed, someone said. Buzzed had a whole different meaning to my generation, but okay. Everything about him was a sort of steel gray with a touch of rust.

He rarely moved unless shuffling to a meal, but his eyes betrayed that there was not stillness inside him. They darted from the day room to the main door, up and down the hallways, back again. Repeat. Always watching for trouble. The Lookout.

He greeted me with a small bow each morning. Followed by a warning. Or a promise. I was never entirely sure which it was. His throat spilled gravel when he spoke, the rumbling tones lifted with the music of his accent like a stone bird someone carved on a Roman wall in a time long ago and now stuck in a history book.

He had no teeth left. Maybe that's why he didn't smile much.

"Anyone give you a hard time, anyone not respectful, any of these gonzos take a liberty, you come tell me. I'll take the care of them." Each morning he then placed his right hand, laid flat, into his mouth; his gray-tinged gums clamping down on his hand which he then flung out in a sharp upward swoop.

Despite the lack of teeth, there was a sincere menace in the gesture. I always thanked him politely, and assured him that his fellow patients had been gentlemen. He usually muttered under his breath in response. The only word I could confidently translate was bastardi.

I checked into the wood and glass box that was the nurses' station, to note that I was there on time. The head nurse always eyed me sourly, as if she would transform into a happy women if only I was NOT there. All summer long. Never cracked a smile and, unlike my gallant sentry, she possessed teeth. I saw them. Although she did not say the words, she made it clear that she did not consider me an asset to her ward. When they tote it all up later, she probably wouldn't be the only one thumbs down on our experiment. Over the summer, fully half of the teenage experiments that started with me vanished. That's a lot of drop-outs.

Early on, I was almost a drop-out. When my father heard that I had been assigned to a locked men's ward, he threatened to call the program and demand that I be transferred to a women's ward. I could be as stubborn as he was. I begged him not to humiliate me like that. I told him that I would rather quit. My father didn't believe in quitting. I think, in the end, after he caved, he thought that I was being brave. In reality, I was more afraid of the dull, lifeless, women that I had seen shuffling back and forth to the women's ward. If I was unlucky enough, I could become one of those women one day. That thought, and the women who represented that possible future, terrified me.

After checking in at the nurses' station, I began sliding into my usual hangout, the dayroom, but first I made the mistake of observing and speaking.

"It looks like Mr. Mc Elderry has joined the group," I said. For the past two weeks, he paced the ward, keeping the others at bay. Now he sat with them watching television, on the fringes of the group, but there.

"Mc Elderry," the Head Nurse sharply corrected my pronunciation. "There is no letter A in Mc."

She pronounces his name like MICK-elderly, only without the second letter l. The patient himself pronounces it MACK-eldairy. I'd read Ken Kesey's *One Flew Over the Cuckoo's Nest*, and silently said "Of course, Nurse Ratchet."

I shrugged, not willing to give her any sign of agreement, thinking the man might not be well, but ought to know his own name. He was somewhere in middle age, not nearly as old as the Italian hall monitor, but old enough to be somebody like a teacher or a priest. One of his hands was in a cast with a metal pin sticking out of it. He told me he broke it punching a cinderblock wall.

"And that's not even the stupidest thing I've ever done," he said with a full-throated laugh.

He had a great laugh, seeming to come up from a place deep inside and spilling out in all satdirections. I didn't ask what other stupid things he had done. Usually, I just waited for the patients to tell me things. They pretty much always told me things.

As I entered the dayroom, most of the men sat in front of a television hung high on the wall, watching a local morning television show that usually bored me. Mr. S, the new guy, left his spot by the window to approach me for a light. What a strange feeling that was. It had stayed strange all summer how these grown men were allowed to smoke their cigarettes, if they had them, but had to come to me or one of the aides for a light. Patients were not allowed matches or a lighter. Being a trusted adult who provides lights to men older than me, some by decades, was such a power shift. I figured one of them could start a fire with a lit cigarette, if they really wanted to that is. So far, nobody wanted to waste the smoke.

Then Mr. Teddy approached me, not for a smoke. He didn't smoke. He liked to be healthy. Mr. Teddy was the opposite of Little Old Italian Guy. If Little Old Italian Guy was, well, really little, Mr. Teddy was big in pretty much every way. For starters, he beamed smiles like sunlight through the metal grids on the windows. I had never seen a happier-looking man, like a black Santa Clause, without the 'Ho, Ho, Ho' stuff.

The funny thing is, though he was always dressed head-to-toe in brown, from his scuffed brown shoes to his brown plaid shirts, he reminded me of a rainbow. One way he was like Little Old Italian Guy is that he'd been there the whole summer. Another was that he, too, had a routine.

"How are you this morning, Mr. Teddy?"

"Just fine, Miss. And a fine day it is. Feeling good."

"I'm so glad to hear that."

"But I need to know..." Of course he did,

Every day he needed to know how to stay fine. He was very concerned about his vitamin intake. I knew what question was coming, and I had prepared, been to the library, taken out books, studied so that I could responsibly answer his daily question. I didn't want to lie to the man. Still, I gave him the respect of waiting for the question anyway.

"But I need to know what vitamin is good for me."

"You know, I think you'd like Vitamin K. You find it in green foods."

"My momma used to cook me greens."

"Yes, like that. Not just collard greens and spinach, but broccoli, too. Vitamin K is good for bones and blood."

"Ah, thank you, Miss. I'll be sure to keep that in mind." He bobbed a nod and shuffled off. I'd run out of vitamins to talk about weeks ago. I had been recycling my nutrition information for a while. If he ever noticed, I guessed he was too polite to say anything.

I took an empty seat in front of the television. The hosts introduced the next guest. "Now, let's welcome the woman known as The Hottest Blaze in Burlesque, Miss Blaze Starr."

There was a little ripple of interest in the room, an energy buzz that was often squelched before it 'got out of control.' but this time the TV channel was not changed. The aide in the room was the easier-going one, the "one of the guys" type. His co-worker, who was built like a side of beef and never mingled much, stayed over by the nurses' station. The Head Nurse smiled at him, a lot, showing teeth. Anyway, it seemed the coast was clear for a little excitement.

Blaze Starr was getting kinda old by then, but still had her famous hourglass figure. The television was black-and-white, of course, color TV's being expensive, so her famous red hair didn't jump off the screen. Much of the early conversation on the show centered around her recent business move, buying the Two O'clock Club where she first came to fame.

Then the host asked her to demonstrate "for all the house-wives out there" how to titillate their mates simply by removing a glove. Heads around me moved closer to the screen. A glove? It seemed that men were pretty easy to titillate, although maybe only the ones confined to dayrooms.

Blaze Starr, staring into the screen with a smokey look in her eyes, ran her fingers up her arm as if she was both stroking a pet cat and was herself the pet cat all in one. Her gloves were long and white like a prom.

The young man sitting next to me was Sharp-Dressed Guy, who was probably closest to my own age among all the patients. His age and his silk shirts made a strange combination. He turned to me, "Would you do that?"

I looked at him, but he wasn't flirting with me or being gross. A simple question.

"Sure, I take off gloves every winter. Although, not quite like that."

Now Blaze began peeling that glove from her arm. Slowly.

"No," he said. Calmly. Purposefully. "Would you do that?"

Blaze was now tugging on the fingers of the glove with her teeth. Short, sharp, movements that somehow made her smile. I realized that he was asking me something that had nothing to do with the television show. Nothing to do with a white glove. He was asking me if I would be a stripper.

"No. No, I couldn't." It would kill my mother.

"What if you didn't have a choice? What if people were counting on you?"

I didn't know why Sharp-Dressed Guy was in the hospital, though I knew the part of the county he came from, a neighborhood that didn't make you think of silk shirts. I began to realize that he wasn't really talking about me.

This was serious. I took a breath. "It would be awfully hard if people were counting on me. I know I sure wouldn't want to have to do that."

He nodded.

We sat in silence for a while as Blaze finished up, twirling the glove before tossing it at the TV screen. One patient lurched forward as if he could catch it.

Sharp-Dressed Guy's voice got flat. "They're releasing me tomorrow."

Usually, patients sounded happy about this. Usually, I'd say something like "Congratulations." But Sharp-Dressed Guy didn't sound happy about it, so I simply said, "Oh."

"I wish they'd keep me." He stood and walked away as they cut to a commercial break.

I had never before heard a patient say that they wished the hospital would keep them. I knew that Sharp-dressed Guy wasn't from a rich neighborhood. I didn't know what he had to do to make the kind of money that bought silk shirts, but I now knew that he didn't really want to do it anymore. And that, probably, he would end up doing it anyway.

The next day, back on the ward, my morning routines of Little Old Italian Guy and Mr. Teddy played out like they always do. This time, though, seeing me talking to Mr. Teddy triggered Head Nurse, who tapped on the glass and motioned me over.

"Take a seat. I see you were talking with Mr. Teddy," she began crossly, as if that wasn't exactly what my job asked me to do. "What do you talk about?"

This woman who didn't like me was demanding to know the content of my conversations. Ugh. But since there apparently was no such thing as a private conversation on a hospital ward, I told her how we usually talked about health and, especially, nutrition.

"Well, stop it," she snapped. I was really confused. My face probably showed it. She put her pen down on the desk, as if explaining something to me took such a monumental effort it required all of her energy. "Because he isn't eating properly any more. He goes to meals and only wants to eat the foods you tell him to eat."

Me? He wasn't eating because of me? I didn't know what to make of that. I was only trying to be helpful, to have an honest conversation. A corner of my heart broke hearing that Mr. Teddy had not been eating because of our little conversations about vitamins. I got that feeling you get when the pinch of your nose begins to hurt and you have to swallow hard, but I was determined not to cry.

"Okay," I said, bracing myself for worse.

She didn't say another word, just turned her head, picked her pen up, and began reading some paper on her desk. I figured I should get out of there.

I couldn't sleep that night, running over and over in my head what I should do about Mr. Teddy. I had spent the day avoiding him, trying to look busy, walking in the wrong direction, but I could feel his puzzled eyes follow me.

Finally, I figured it out and fell asleep.

When I arrived at work the next day, Mr. Teddy rushed up to me, as if he was afraid I would try to slip away.

"Morning, Miss. How are you this morning?"

"I'm good, Mr. Teddy. How are you?"

"Fine, fine. But I need to know –"

I let his question play out, confident that I had a good answer for him.

"Well, you know, I've been thinking. Every vitamin does something good for you. The important thing is to have a balanced diet. If you eat some of whatever the cafeteria offers, you'll get lots of different vitamins."

Mr. Teddy nodded vigorously. "Good. Good."

Pleased with myself, I moved on into the dayroom. A couple of the men approached me about playing a card game.

"Sure," I said. "See if you can get a fourth. Ask Mr. S." Mr. S spent most of his time alone, staring out the window.

We four headed to the card room across the hall from the nurses' station. It was a quiet spot and just big enough to hold a table and some chairs and mirrored the nurses' station with wooden walls halfway up and windows at the top half.

We weren't allowed to gamble or play games like poker or blackjack that might remind people of gambling. The Head Nurse called those games "unsavory," which made me kinda smile because those were my father's favorite card games, and he was the least unsavory person I knew.

At the last minute, Mr. Mc Elderry decided to tag along. This was a different version of Mr. Mc Elderry. Like he was hopped up on something, literally hopping from one foot to the next. Not all anxious-like 'cause he was laughing.

He didn't take his seat at the table. The men began shuffling the deck and dealing cards for gin rummy. I always thought it was odd that a card game named after two types of alcohol was not unsavory, but it wasn't my job to decide what was good or bad.

Mr. Mc Elderry circled the table, looking over everyone's shoulders at their cards, whistling and breaking into song, even doing a little shuffle step.

"Cut it out, Mack." One of the men covered his cards. "You gonna play or just be a pain in the ass?"

"Language in front of the lady," one of the other guys said.

Mr. Mc Elderry suddenly stopped behind me. Without a word of warning, he grabbed the back of my chair, pulling it abruptly onto just the two back legs, and began lowering me and the chair down toward the ground.

"Come on, Mr. Mc Elderry," I said, staring up at the ceiling light. "That's not funny. Put my chair back."

He didn't put me back upright. Just started laughing. That deep belly laugh didn't sound so fun now. Not now that I could feel my heart beating a little faster as fear started licking the backs of my eyes.. Suppose he dropped the chair, even just by accident, and I went smashing to the floor? That would probably hurt. Maybe break something.

I tried to keep my cool. We were friendly. He wouldn't mean to hurt me. "Come on. Don't do this. Put me – "

Suddenly there was a rush of energy in the room, a really loud bang against the wall behind me, followed by a second bang, and a third as the two front legs met the floor in a rush and my chest bumped hard against the tabletop, sending cards flying. The beefy aide quickly restrained Mr. Mc Elderry in a kind of police hold, then shoved him out of the card room door. When I got up to look after them, I saw them heading down the hall toward the isolation rooms. My eyes met with those of the Head Nurse. She glared at me.

My guardian, Little Old Italian Guy, was not at his post.

Suddenly it was Thursday, my penultimate day on the job. Mr. Mc Elderry was out of solitary, but was much changed. Sitting off by himself, he seemed sleepy, medicated. I'd read this play before I came to work here. It's set in a French insane asylum ages ago and has the tremendous name of *The Persecution and Assassination of Jean-Paul Marat as Performed by the Inmates of the Asylum of Charenton Under the Direction of the Marquis de Sade*. I thought the title was too cool. They made a movie out of it, but my parents wouldn't let me see it. Probably because of the Marquis de Sade's reputation. Or maybe because of the *Catholic Review*.

Anyway, the asylum in that play was a wild place. By comparison, my summer had been tame. Up until yesterday. I still felt guilty about Mr. Mc Elderry being punished like that, could still hear the bang of his body being shoved against the wall, could still see him frog-marched down the hall. Here, this morning, Mr. Mc Elderry appeared to still be paying the price.

Head Nurse beckoned me with a wave of her hand. Taking a deep breath, I prepared myself for getting chewed out over what happened at the card game. The attack came from an entirely different direction.

"I distinctly told you to stop discussing vitamins with Mr. Teddy." She picked up her pen and began thumping it against the desk while glaring at me with a look that said she would rather be thumping my head.

"I stopped telling him about different vitamins."

"Well, you told him something." She paused long enough that I felt the need to say something.

"I only –"

Her voice cut through my words, scattering them. "You only what? Because in the shower this morning, it was discovered that he had bits of different foods, wrapped in napkin tissue or toilet paper, little bits of food all over his body."

What? My brain had trouble with the picture forming there.

"That poor man had bits of rotting food all over him. What do you have to say for yourself?"

"I just told him to eat some of everything he was offered. That way he would have a balanced diet." I had thought the problem was solved. So wrong.

When the lecture was finally over, I slipped back into the dayroom. I hadn't spoken to Mr. S since the card game disaster. Approaching him at his usual spot by the window, I noticed that he looked different. There was something, oh, kinda hard to say, but some sense that he was no longer entirely solid. Not quite like a ghost, not like he could pass through solid objects. But if he could, he might pass through the metal grates guarding the window he stared out, much like the white smoke he exhaled.

I heard him sigh as I came closer. A heavy, back-of-the-throat, sigh. No, not smoke, maybe more like the opposite, that he was so weighed down by whatever thoughts pulled at his mind that he stood rooted at the window by pain, not choice.

"Hey, Mr. S," I said softly. "How ya doing?"

"Oh, I'm fine." His expression told that for a lie. "I owe you an apology for the other day."

"Me? Whatever for?"

"I didn't stick up for you at the card game. Worthless."

What the heck? "I don't know why there was such a fuss. I was fine." I felt another pang about Mr. Mc Elderry getting into trouble. "Why they had to overreact..."

"Why? Because you're a little girl. He is a grown man. A big one, but that doesn't excuse me from doing nothing." Hanging his head, his voice dropped to a whisper. "Useless as usual."

Frustration at being treated like a silly, useless child for much of the summer hit hard. "I was fine. He was never trying to hurt me. Why doesn't anybody trust me?" I pushed down the thought of Mr. Teddy and the tissue-wrapped food.

"I've failed again," he said, following his own thoughts away from mine. "Looking back over my life, all I see is a litter of failure. Come tomorrow, a half-century of failure."

"Come tomorrow?"

"I turn 50 tomorrow. And look what I got to show for it."
Waving with his cigarette hand, he gestured toward the room.

What an awful way to celebrate your birthday. In the whole
summer, I realized, there had never been a party on the ward.
Could it really be that all summer no one ever had a birthday? Or
were things like birthdays just not celebrated?

"Fifty's not so old."

He gave me a look that said he knew I was lying.

Flailing to defend myself, I said, "Well, it's middle-aged."

"I guess you could say that. Except I won't live to a hundred.
Drank too much. Beat up my body." He slumped as if he wanted
to disappear. I couldn't think of anything to say that didn't
sound like a lie, so I just stood there with him.

That night, my father asked me why I was so sad. Was it
because tomorrow was my last day at work? I explained about
Mr. S. Only I left out all the stuff about Mr. Mc Elderry because
my father would probably overreact to it, too. I just told him
about the birthday.

After dinner, my father went out to run some errands. He
came home with one of the small birthday cakes from Silber's
bakery. One with flowers and Happy Birthday written on it.

WHEN I WENT to the asylum the next morning, I held the
bakery box tight to my chest, but not in an attempt to hide it.
The girl who caused so much trouble over food wasn't letting
this box of food go easily. I didn't stop to talk to Old Italian Guy.
I walked purposely past the nurses station into the day room,
where I knew I would find Mr. S standing in his spot by the
window.

"This is for you," I said, thrusting the small, white box toward him.

He gave me a puzzled look, but took the box and slowly lifted the lid. He silently stared at the cake inside ... for too long.

"I'm sorry I couldn't bring a knife, but, well, you know. I was thinking that you could take it to lunch and they could cut it for you."

He finally looked up at me. His eyes were wet. Had I screwed up?

"I'm sorry it doesn't have your name on it, but confidentiality and all. And I can't do candles because, well, they're pretty touchy about fire and all——"

"It's perfect." His voice was just a whisper.

Relief. "Oh, good. Happy Middle Age!"

He smiled, just a little, still with the tears. "I've never had a birthday cake before."

Never had a birthday cake before? In fifty years. The sentence sliced clean through me. Not even as a boy? Never once did someone love him enough to bake or buy a cake? Fifty years. I knew, beyond a shadow of doubt, that if I had been handed his life, then I would be crazy, too.

THE REINVENTION INTERVENTION
FRANCESCA MCBELL

When her colleagues stage an intervention to pull her out of self-doubt, a young woman is thrust into a false identity, leading her to a deeper understanding of her true self.

Francesca McBell is project manager for an art and nature park, a romance writer, and a former college professor. When she's not working, she throws pottery and enjoys spending time with her family.

PLAYLIST

This is Me Trying — **Taylor Swift**
Breathe — **Lin-Manuel Miranda**
I'm a Loser — **The Beatles**

Scan to listen at buttonhall.com/books/left-turns

pace around my small office like a zoo animal, rearranging
the leaves on my fake olive tree every few turns. But they
snap back into place as if even the consideration of change is
too much for them. It's not the most glamorous of faculty
offices, given its location in the basement and all. But, this wing
of the school has been recently renovated and, on top of that, it's
a bit harder to find for students. Which is why I volunteered to
take this space.

Students are wandering the hallways. I hear them chattering
away as they escape their classrooms. They sound energized and
exhausted at the same time, like Red Bull poured into warm
milk. My ex once accused me of disliking students. That's definitely not the case. I adore them, and maybe, just maybe, I'm a
bit intimidated by them. I pause behind my door, and, for the
sake of honesty, listen in. There's grumbling about grades, it's the
last day before summer after all, and talk about cute boys and–I
gulp–there's my name. They are talking about me. But before I
can make out anything of substance, the litany of students has
been shoved out of hearing range and I'm left with nothing but
self-doubt to ponder how they critique my teaching, grading,
and advising.

I take a piece of blotting paper from the desk and lean over
the small mirror, dabbing away the tiny sweat pearls that are
gathering on my forehead. At least I'm still cute, or so they say. I
have no French ancestors whatsoever, but people tend to assume
that Napoleon's blood runs through my veins, which explains
why I am short, olive-skinned and hazel-eyed. Therefore, I must
be someone very stylish and cultural. Maybe that's why I've been
able to hold on to this job for years. Maybe people think there is
more behind that very French façade.

I drop the paper when three small knocks land on my door.
Then, without hesitation, my department chair, Corrie, walks in.

She furrows her brows. "You're not driving yourself crazy about this again, are you?"

I wipe my palms against the seams of my jacket. "It's a bloody teaching evaluation. It's a big deal." I wish I did have Napoleon's bravery instead of his ancestral looks.

Even though Corrie closes her eyes, I can see her rolling them inside her head. "It's a formality. I know, and Henrik knows, that you're a good professor."

A formality that my job depends on...

"Henrik?" Henrik is a math professor with several awards under his belt and charisma that makes even the most arithmophobic students consider majoring in numbers. "I thought Martin was my other judge." This is one of the consequences of being at a small college, you might get evaluated by someone outside your department.

Corrie picks up my water bottle from the desk and pushes it into my hand. "Annabelle," she mothers up her voice. "We've discussed this before. We're not judges ... we're colleagues. It's going to be fine. Drink some water ... or something stronger."

Wouldn't that be a hoot? An underqualified AND tipsy marketing professor. The university would have a ball at their next after-hours drink night. I take a sip from my water bottle.

Corrie rests her hand on the doorknob and answers as if she heard my internal monologue. "I really wonder who gave you permission to go down this impostor route. Anyways, let's get this formality over with. Tonight you'll come over to my place and we'll celebrate the almost-end of the semester."

I give the plastic tree one more shake before I follow her to my eval– nope, can't do it, my judgment day.

AN HOUR of teaching blur and another of deep breathing exercises later, I stare into the antique mirror that I found at a flea market a few Sundays back. It fits perfectly into my tiny foyer with its classy and yet romantic white frame. I wish I could find a place where I'd fit in so seamlessly. It isn't (and never was) in a classroom, that much I know. I'd known it since the day I started teaching. Others are slow to catch on. But, maybe they did this afternoon?

Back in grad school, I landed my first, highly competitive, teaching assistantship. Nobody around me was better prepared. I knew all the marketing research and strategies like the back of my personalized talisman. But not even the golden frog I carried day in and day out in my pocket could help me with that first round of students. I presented my aesthetically appealing PowerPoint side-by-side with my honed lecture. But it took less than three minutes before questions popped up from the crowd. Questions that neither my textbooks nor my internships had prepared me for. I got flustered, and told the student who was bombarding me with questions that I, truthfully, didn't have the answer. First came the look of disappointment from him. My stomach sank. Then I caught my advisor in the back row shaking her head in disapproval and mouthing "Wing it." I managed to get through the lesson, winging it left and right. But I knew at that moment that I would never truly belong here, never have the answers to fulfill the enthusiastic curiosity of eager humans trying to learn from me. ME! Ever since, I've been waiting for someone to officially call me out on my BS.

There was a moment in class today when I saw, back in the room from the "judge's panel," Henrik's mouth twitch as if he'd eaten something that was supposed to be delicious but ended up being a dud. I try to mimic his expression in the mirror, but I'm not a good mime, either. I do manage to give myself a disappointed smirk. Was that how he felt about my teaching? Why else would he make a face like that?

I pull out the silk scarf that I had woven clumsily into my hair and start over. It gets stuck in a painful knot, and now I have to untie every single strand of hair. But at least it wins me some time.

I don't want to go to Corrie's party. I don't want to go anywhere. I want to stay in this apartment, watch a rom-com, and drink some of the boxed wine that's sitting in my fridge from last weekend's building meeting. I don't care for wine but I'll take it over going to the store. And I prefer it over going to Corrie's. Even though I love her. She's the best boss and I am grateful for her. My colleagues, who are also lovely and all better teachers than I am, will certainly talk about my evaluation, and tell me dozens of times how everything will be just splendid. Of course, there's no way they could know this, given the fact that the official judgment won't be released until all exams are graded, turned in, and the semester is officially declared over. Which is soon, thankfully. Or maybe regretfully, since it might be my last day of employment.

Come to think of it, Henrik's mouth was really more of a frown than a twitch. I refrain from trying to copy him this time and finish my hairdo. Then, I force myself into doing mode. I won't disappoint Corrie, of course not. She's putting together this little meetup to relax me, and I'm ashamed to even be thinking about backing out and letting her down. And maybe, after I collect my well-meant pats on the back, I'll find some distraction. I do remember a fun party there, where everyone ended up playing foosball. I make a mental note to suggest that later, then I drop my keys in the brown leather bag and march out the door, spending the time of my short walk making discussion topic lists in my head.

Corrie lives in a small, blue townhouse nestled in the old part of town. It's the kind of neighborhood where it seems like everybody knows each other—they meet on their morning dog walks, borrow sugar from each other, and give spare keys to whoever lives next to them. But when I shared this fantasy with Corrie last year, she broke out into laughter. "Anabelle," she shook her head while still trying to control her laughing fit, "you have to stop believing that things are always the way they seem to be ... to you. My neighbor is a guy I've never met but I already despise because he's renting the place out as an Airbnb and most of his guests are annoying as f***."

"Maybe I prefer my version," I responded, slightly nervous that she had painted me as naïvee. Which I can be, but I better not show that to the person who is literally in charge of my career.

No, *I am*, of course. Never mind.

"Then maybe you should stop trying to control other people's version of you. Never works. Everyone makes up their own shit," she wiggled her eyebrows and I have thought about that conversation only about twice a day for the last year. But isn't that what we're meant to control? Aren't we supposed to put our best foot forward so our bosses, neighbors, and students see the shining light instead of the basement dimmer? I guess the jury is still out.

I hear steps behind me now and automatically quicken my pace.

"Annabelle, wait up." Martin's voice is hoarse against the background traffic noise.

I pause and turn to him. "There's a relief! I thought you were some stalker or something."

He laughs and adjusts his tweed cap. "Not in this picturesque piece of the city."

Our steps fall into an amicable cadence. "Speaking of the opposite of stalking, why did you abandon me today?" I add a wide smile so that he knows I'm not really upset.

"Apologies," he says. "I had a small medical procedure scheduled and it was complicated to move it so ..."

"Oh my," I interrupt, ashamed to have brought it up. "I hope everything's okay?"

He waves me off. "No big deal. But Henrik was happy to fill in, so... all good?"

All good? That's a question I can almost certainly answer with a resounding NO. Dude, I had a career breaking evaluation today so how could everything, EVERYTHING, be good? "I guess we'll know when I get my feedback." I shrug.

He chuckles. "I see."

Generally, I rely on people to reassure me when I say something doomsday-y. So I'm not sure what exactly to do with an "*I see*". But now we're in front of Corrie's ornately carved door.- Martin uses the Irish trinity knot door knocker heartily, as if he's alerting the Airbnb guests, too, of our arrival.

Corrie greets us in the same loud fashion as the knock and I wish for my couch again. Maybe the end of the semester makes my colleagues feel boisterous and bold while I am filled with the desire to hide under a blanket. I think I'd be very happy with a couple of cats if it wasn't for my unfortunate allergy blockade.

"Whatcha thinking?" Corrie asks while Martin slips by her into the living room.

"That cat ladies have a bad rep for no good reason." I hand her my coat with a "Thanks," then slip off my boots.

Corrie nods solemnly. "Your predecessor had such a love of cats that students swore they'd get better grades if they included cat pics in their PowerPoints. Maybe we should pass it on to the sociology department as a research topic. Let's go in."

I follow her. The house is cozy and, if it weren't for the post-cards with feminist quotes stuck behind random pictures and mirror frames, reads more like the home of a grandma who likes her needlepoint and pottery. And suddenly I'm glad I came. This is a nice place with nice people and why in the world shouldn't it be a nice evening? I'm not going to allow myself to doomsday a harmless happy hour. My ex used to say that "Not everything is about you, Annabelle. Most of the time, people just want to hang out and have a drink and they're not concerned with even one aspect of your life." He was right, somewhat. I couldn't get over the tone he said this in—a slightly snarky, mostly I'm-so-much-wiser-than-you attitude—but his basic message was probably spot on. Why would my work friends spend their time figuring out my career moves? They have their own issues. Not as dire as mine, but still existent. Probably. Whatever.

When I enter the living room, I know immediately that my little self-pep-talk had been as much bullshit as I, deep down, knew it was. Corrie, who has gracefully slipped by me, Henrik, Martin, and Pearl from the Vet Tech department are standing in front of the purple, button-tufted sofa. They are lined up like soldiers, not talking to each other but staring at me. Their teeth are glinting in the light of the Tiffany lamp, but I can't tell if those pearlies are smiles or threats. I freeze in my tracks.

I think there's a ten second or ten minute pause—time is hard to tell in these circumstances—where nobody moves. Then Pearl steps forward. She laughs in a partially forced fashion and takes my hand.

"Oh, baby," she says, and I follow her to the seating arrange-ment like a puppet. "We scared you." She pushes me into the blue, velvet chair and shakes her head. "I told you guys she'd be scared."

There's too much mention of the word scare, as if I'm simultaneously meant to be and not meant to be frightened. They'd know I'd go with the latter. Apparently, they've discussed my reaction. I know I keep staring at them, but I don't know what to say or do. Running away is a good option, but also too childish. I'd never recover from that.

"It's okay, doll," Pearl pats my shoulder and sinks onto the couch. If Corrie is my boss at work, then Pearl is my work mother. She's always talking about retiring, but she might stay longer at the school than the rest of us. And right now, she reminds me of my own mother when I missed my curfew by over an hour in my teenage years.

What did I do? I try to speak but my voice is not cooperating. Everybody's now sitting, but there's no doubt left in my mind that this is not a harmless party to decompress but rather a get-together about me. Are they all here to console me on my teaching disaster? Is this the way to tell me I'm fired and then get me drunk? These thoughts help me to muster enough anger to balance out my fear as I rediscover my vocal chords. "What is happening?" The words come out clipped and machine-like.

"Well," Corrie straightens the lacy table runner, "we wanted to talk to you."

Talk to me? That seems like the understatement of the century. "About me being fired?"

Henrik squints at me as if I'm a preschooler. "No," he says and gestures to Martin to pour everyone wine. "About that."

"That?" The hairs on my neck are standing up straight. Maybe they are also gathering to tell me something.

"Yes," he sounds exhausted, and I'm sweating now. I never want to exhaust others. I want to make them happy. Or, at a minimum, not bother them. But he goes on, "About your constant state of self-doubt and ensuing panic."

"It's called 'impostor syndrome', honey." Pearl pats my hand as if I'm a patient just waking up from surgery. Then she pushes a glass of wine into my it. "And yours has gotten a bit out of hand."

Ah yes. Impostor syndrome. Even my high school counselor was zeroed in on that. I relax a tiny bit. If the point here is to hand me that diagnosis, they will be let down. I accepted this feeling long ago as a natural companion. I take a sip of the red, not caring what it tastes like. But it's rather bitter. "Maybe it's not imposter if it's true."

"Nonsense," Corrie waves me off as if this isn't even up for discussion. "And yours needs to stop. It's swallowing you whole."

I shake my head, feeling more and more in my element now. "I think I just need to work a bit harder, prepare a bit better, and get a few more years of work experience. It will go away." I cross my fingers to my heart. "Unless I failed today's teaching eval."

Martin lets out an audible breath. "You are smarter and more prepared than most, but –" he holds up his hand when he notices that I'm inclined to interrupt him– "but it doesn't matter how often we tell you that. We decided that something else needs to happen. A wake-up call."

"You decided that?" I must have missed the moment when I signed my life over to them.

Corrie grins at me. "It's an intervention, Annabelle. It's meant to push you. And nobody but you will make the final decision. But we sure hope you trust us enough to go with that..."

"And where are you pushing me to? Is there 'Imposter Rehab'?" I can't help but picture a hospital-like space filled with people who doubt that they have good enough imposter syndrome to belong there. It could be a fun comic.

"Kind of," Pearl smiles widely and I notice amusement all around now. My colleagues are obviously more than excited to present this plan to me. Or maybe they have the same comical place in mind that I do.

I swallow. There would be no reason to do this unless it would mean discomfort.

"We've found a place where you truly will be an imposter," Henrik nods towards his wine glass and I'm trying to decipher this.

"*In vino veritas*?" I try.

"*In vino impostorem*." He's now in full celebration mode. "Pearl's cousin owns a restaurant one town over. Their sommelier quit. We signed you up as his replacement for the summer."

I'm trying to repeat the words in my head ... but nope. They make not an ounce of sense. "What?" I squint against the lamp. "How much did you all drink before I arrived?"

"See?" Pearl takes the lead. "As far as we can tell, you know zilch about wine—well maybe the difference between red and white. You don't even like the stuff, really. So, go in there and pretend the crap out of it. Be a real imposter and experience what being an imposter really feels like. Have fun with it. The worst that can happen is that someone gets a wine they don't like."

I did not see this coming. Even in my wildest imagination. The rehab idea seems, all of the sudden, like a desirable option. "You want me to do what?" Am I dreaming? I'm not even certain how to pronounce sommelier correctly. There goes my French advantage.

Corrie recalls the plan patiently. In a nutshell, I'm supposed to be a sommelier, the 'R' is definitely silent, in a restaurant to experience what it means to be a true imposter and—AND—have FUN with it.

I close my eyes, open them again. Nope, not a dream. "And what would be the point again, besides bad customer service? I missed that."

Martin leans back into the plush seat. "Once you see what it's like to be a true fraud, we think you'll gain the confidence to trust yourself and your abilities. You'll see how amazing you really are."

Then it's Henrik's turn. "Annabelle, we love you. Think of this as professional development to be the good professor we see in you. When I watched you today, I saw how you were subtly sabotaging your own brilliance. If you don't do this, I cannot put in my recommendation for you to stay. And if you don't do this, you'll never have the confidence to do any of the amazing things we *know* you're capable of."

So that's what those fifty-or-so facial contortions were.

"Oh, and your first shift starts in an hour," Corrie says, rather nonchalantly given the urgency of the words. "C'mon, I'm driving."

And with that, my fate seems decided.

THE RESTAURANT IS SMALL, quaint, and cozy. It's nestled into a new-ish neighborhood, between experimental theaters, music venues, and health food stores. I don't know anyone who lives around here, and I assume my friends, or fiends—the jury is still out—chose this spot because of it. After some good cries and little tantrums, I accepted this challenge. Not because I'm convinced it will heal my feeling of being sub-par in my career, but because I DO need a break. A change of scenery. A vacation.

It would be nice if I could simply be a guest here. The red door looks inviting, and when I open it, I find myself in a little waiting space. A heavy maroon curtain keeps the air, and me, out of the eating area. It's like I'm being transported back to the holding area before an exam. It's the worst part, truly, the waiting. Time given to you, without request, to ponder all the whys of why you should turn around and run. But before I can escape, the curtain gets pulled back by a strong, and a bit hairy hand and a giant man appears. His dark curls are held back with a washed out bandana. He's wearing a black t-shirt and his arms sparkle with sweat.

"You Belle?" He asks and holds out his hand.

Belle, right. That's my imposter name. This way, Corrie explained, I wouldn't have to feel like a complete liar, only like the 95% kind, and, if things do get out (oh please, don't let them), I have one less thing to explain. Even though I doubt this bodybuilder man in front of me, who I assume to be the owner, would care about my name if I confessed to this whole scam. Maybe I should tell him now?

But instead, I just nod while he grabs my hand with a firm, safe grip. This guy definitely does not suffer from feeling ungrounded.

"Hi," I say. "Yes. Yes, I'm Belle. Belle. Nice to meet you ..."

"I'm Louie." He releases my hand and ushers me into the cramped space behind the curtain. There are maybe ten small tables smushed in here, plus a few seats at the bar. When every spot is taken, I assume nobody can move.

"Nice place," I say. My voice sounds childish and, maybe it's Louie's name or his easy smile, but right then and there I decide to fully commit. I'm here, and I'll dive in. For however long I can swim.

"Thanks, it's doing pretty well. We tend to get quite the eclectic bunch. There's a fine line between artists and the need to be fully dialed in to every bite they eat and every sip they take." He grins and points at the wall of wine behind the bar, which seems to be built of old train rails. I gulp looking at all the labels that tell me nothing.

"And that's why we need a somm. Can I take your coat?"

"So that I can dial their taste buds in?" I peel myself out of my light summer jacket and hand it to him. It's warm enough to go without layers, but I figured wearing a jacket would give me a bit more of a professional look. I already regret showing up in my rather conservative light blue button-down shirt. This place calls for more ... flair.

He walks through the swinging doors into the kitchen, and I follow. "Taste buds or beliefs about food?" He continues to the sparkling clean row of ovens, sinks, and counter space into another room behind it. There's a TV, a couch, and a card table with chairs. He hangs my coat over a chairback. "Even though I'm a chef, and I prepare them here every day, I have not once understood why anyone needs to eat oysters. And why some people might like them. I would bet that the majority like the image of them much more than the slimy mouthfeel."

I laugh. We're definitely on the same page about these so-called delicacies. "So, you're feeding people's minds, brains, and thoughts about themselves?"

This is actually a great concept. I can work with this. At the end of the day, I do know a thing or two about marketing. So, if I can manage to sell them the picture of a wine, the idea of how it might enhance their moment, I might survive for at least an hour. That's my goal. Small steps. Survive one hour.

And I like Louie. He seems so at ease that I wish I could cut off one of his magical locks and take a snippet of that power for myself. I'm trying to remember if I've ever felt at ease, but nothing comes promptly to mind.

"You got it." There's that smile again. "We're a small working crowd here so, once people come in for the dinner rush, it will be hectic."

I nod. "Well, then I better get to work and make sure I know all those wines." I pinch myself. "I mean, not KNOW them, but know which ones you have."

"Sure thing."

Sure nothing. Just two hours to get myself ready for the

imposter challenge. What, besides everything, can go wrong? Thank God for Google and my ability to learn things fast.

———

HECTIC IS the understatement of the century. We're open for thirty minutes, and the place is packed like a Manhattan club and filled even more with non-stop chatter that seems to bridge across the tables. And those sociable guests all want wine. From me. Gulp.

Ahmed, tonight's server, sends me to the window nook where an older couple is beaming at me.

"*Bonjour.* How are you two?"

Judging from his faded Nirvana t-shirt and Gucci reading glasses, I'd place the man in his sixties. He smiles, then says, "Splendid, my dear. We've been trying to snag a table here for the last two weeks and finally got one. Winner, winner." He claps his open hand onto the table with remarkable enthusiasm.

"We're so glad to have you," I sound professional, which is a good start. "What can I help you with?"

"Well," the woman readjusts her gray ballerina bun, then picks up the small menu and points to the oysters. "We're thinking of starting with those. They seem to be a staple of this place."

I can't hold back a smile, thinking of Louie's observations. "They are; and from what I've gathered, people feel great after having them. Chef never stops talking about them!"

"They are an aphrodisiac," the woman blushes confidently. Her skin color now matches her crocheted tank top.

Right. I knew there was something else. "And you'd like a wine that"—I take a deliberate pause while I run through the labels that I've started to research and memorize—"enhances that more?"

"We're in it for the whole experience." The man fists his hand for emphasis. "What's your suggestion?"

I deliver the first label that comes to mind. It has the outline of a couple in an embrace on the label. "I have a lovely Merlot tonight. I think it will give you what you're hoping for."

The woman crinkles her heavily powdered forehead. "A red? Really? I've never heard of serving red wine with fish, let alone with oysters."

Shit. Shitty shit. Instead of trying to memorize the wine list, I probably should have started with reading the menu and figuring out the fitting wines, then I could have stuck to those options. That would have been the more reasonable way to approach this. But now I'm stuck. "I can certainly pour you a lovely white, one that also compliments the oysters." Look at me, making it up as I go. "However," there's fun bubbling up inside of my body and for once, I'm embracing it. "You two do seem to treasure a new experience that puts you just a bit out of your comfort zone. And that's what a nice red could do with your dish. It elevates it. Takes you somewhere new."

You have to love what marketing can do, really. I pause with a quizzical look on my face. Will they bite? And, more importantly, if they do, how will that experiment play out?

"That's brilliant," the man finally says. "I'm starting to see why people rave about this place. Let's do it. Let's open our eyes to new horizons."

I guess that makes three of us. I nod. "Excellent. We can always switch you to a safer white if the route is not where you'd like to travel." I'm turning into a poet here, too. My journey tonight is definitely surreal.

The rest of the night is a blur. I flit between tables, creating story after story about why the wine I suggest is just the one for that guest. Very few patrons challenge me at all, and only one goes against my recommendation.

Louie comes out of the kitchen every so often and mingles. He sends me an amused eyebrow raise when chatting at a table where I served a bubbly rose with their steak dish. It occurs to me a bit later that I never questioned his humor in the small gestures. Not like Henrik's expression at my teaching eval. What is it about being here, that makes me not second-guess my truly uneducated self? Maybe it's best to not over-question this.

At midnight, Ahmed, Louie, and I sink onto the emptied bar stools and Louie opens a bottle of champagne.

"Let's celebrate your first day." He pours the fizzy drink into beer glasses since we're all out of clean champagne flutes. I figured that everyone who came here for a celebratory reason should have champagne with or before their dinner.

Ahmed shakes his head. "You're certainly bringing a new flair to wine. Garnacha with oysters?" He laughs into his glass.

I clink my drink to Louie's. "Just going with the program." If this is my rehab, I'm sticking with it.

He catches my gaze for a sweet moment that makes me think of oysters. "I'm glad you're here. I think you're just what we—what the program—needed."

I take a gulp that's too big, and when the bubbles creep into my nose I laugh-sneeze. "I think you (ahem), the program is what I needed, too."

And just like that, my imposter journey has taken off, full speed.

LOST AND FOUND
KATE JOHNSTON

A woman's obsessive behavior gets her into trouble after her boyfriend inexplicably breaks up with her.

Kate Johnston is a fiction writer whose short stories have appeared in several anthologies including Wolf Warriors, Compass Points, The Green Silk Journal, *and* Wayfaring. *She lives in New Hampshire with her family where she welcomes early mornings as she pens her first novel. When Kate isn't writing, she's baking ooey-gooey desserts or searching for fairies in her backyard. Kate loves all creatures, great and small. And she adores fragments.*

PLAYLIST

I Have Nothing — **Whitney Houston**
Out of Reach — **GABRIELLE**
Brave — **Sara Bareilles**
Unwritten — **Natasha Bedingfield**

Scan to listen at buttonhall.com/books/left-turns

The fire escape ladder had seen better days.

From my precarious position on the rusty, broken rung at the top of the ladder, I tilted my gaze down to the parking lot and the side street one more time. Still no sign of Jake's Audi anywhere. Did he still come home for his lunch break? Probably. That gave me about two hours to snoop through his apartment for my frog.

My frog. Not his. Mine.

Leaning forward, I tried the window. The sash squeaked open, and I exhaled a breath of relief. Leaving a window unlocked was so not Jake, but I bet he figured a fourth-floor apartment and a ladder that had to have failed code were going to scare off intruders.

A step, a lunge, and a heave-ho. I dove in, sprawling across the carpeted floor. Standing and wiping flaking paint and rust from my jean shorts and tank top, I scanned the area. Video gaming equipment. Dumbbells. Flat-screen television. Recliner. LA Lakers memorabilia. Law school books.

My throat tightened. Things he'd once shared with me were here, unpacked. He'd totally moved in. Right now, I could picture our—well, I guess, *my* living room. The space haphazardly arranged because I never reorganized things to cover up the empty spots he'd left behind.

I gently rubbed the smooth leather of his recliner. Grudgingly appreciated there was no rank odor, no empty beer bottles or food-crusted plates anywhere. Only a half-empty water bottle on the coffee table betrayed the otherwise tidy room. Single life was treating him well. Then a little voice piped up asking if I was sure he was still single.

"Shut it," I muttered out loud. It'd only been about a month. Of course he was still single. The threads of my focus began to fray, and I had an overwhelming urge to check his bedroom. No, Fiona, this isn't about you. This is about finding Igor. Be methodical, not whack. Efficient, not scatterbrained. Start here, search thoroughly, then move on to other rooms.

Jake and I had dated almost three years, moved in together six months ago into a tiny but cost-effective one-bedroom apartment in a triplex. We hadn't bothered unpacking most of our crap because we had our eye on a house on Lakeview Boulevard. He'd had a whole plan for us once he made partner at North, Vance, and Adams. His promotion and substantial raise at the law firm combined with my freelance graphic design gigs and scaling back on our spending—we could afford it by the end of the year.

I really thought he was the one. Charming, kind, smart, ambitious, hot with a capital HOT—he had it all. Even Dad liked him. Jake had rescued my heart when I was so sure I'd never find love again. It's because of him that I started believing I could do more with my life—no, no, no, Fiona—what did Sasha from Balance, Bliss, Etc. tell you? I sighed before drawing in a deep breath, hand on heart, connecting to my Inner Goddess. *I do not live through a man. I am complete as my own.*

Still. When you find a guy that checks all the boxes, he's a keeper, right? So—*full disclosure*—when Jake started getting distant, I freaked. Tracked his cell phone. Snooped through his email. Called his mom—yeah, that one was pretty cringy. But when you're thirty-nine and gray hairs are cropping up as quickly as dandelions, freaking out over a wobbly relationship seems like a logical reaction.

Jake ended things and moved out on the sly. I was with a client when our downstairs neighbor left a message on my voice mail complaining that all the activity was disturbing her yoga routine. Wasn't till I got home that evening that I saw his things were gone.

He left money for the next month's rent plus utilities on the counter, and I couldn't decide between distress or anger. He just walked out? With no explanation? Even though I'd sensed that things were off, I hadn't fully prepared myself for worst-case scenario. How could I be so naïve?

Because I was too wrapped up in his perfection, his put-togetherness, his stability. Somehow, he made spreadsheets and gaming sexy. He was the level head to my free spirit. Jake knew all the ways to make me—oh, Lord.

Get a hold of yourself, Fiona. *Inner Goddess.* Inn. Er. Godd. Ess.

Now, where the hell is my frog?

I moved inch-by-inch through Jake's living room, irked to find he'd bought himself some temperamental orchids and succulents he had no business raising. I mean, he had every right to own plants, he just didn't know a thing about how to take care of them. Jake's green thumb was better directed toward money.

Hold up. What possessed him to buy plants, especially the kind way too easy to kill? My gut was swimming until I moved closer and saw the brown, limp foliage. I touched the soil in each pot. Hard as a rock. And they were getting the wrong kind of light. Ha! He had to be single. I frowned at the poor cactus. Jake's single, but his plants are dying.

Shoot. I really didn't have time, but I couldn't ignore their pleas for help. Quickly, I did a little rearranging of furniture and relocated the plants. One by one. Moved them all to a different window. Then I grabbed his water bottle and gave each one a drink. "Hang in there, friends, he might learn eventually." Would Jake notice? Yes. Would he be angry? Yes, but none of that will matter when I find Igor.

I continued my search, opening cabinet doors in the television stand and below the bookcase. Poked through the knick-knacks on the shelves, but my heart rate spiked when I found several framed photos of him and his gorgeousness.

My fingers, of their own accord, found their way to his

image. Stroking him through the glass. I swallowed down the memories that flared. After he'd moved out, I stowed all possible reminders of him because the very idea of him re-shattered me. Photos were the worst culprit of all. But even with the sadness, I scouted each and every picture, hoping hoping *hoping* that just one of them would tell me he hadn't truly left me.

But, no. Not a single photo that included me or of our three years together. However, on the bright side, there were no photos of him with another woman, either. Yes! They were all of his fraternity brothers or his family or his golf team. Some of them I hadn't seen before, like the one of him as a tanned-and-toned teenager at some kind of summer camp. Where had he been keeping them? Not at our place, I was sure of that. They'd probably been in the boxes we'd never unpacked after our move. My fingers were still dancing across his various images. *Enough. Get back to the mission.*

Igor. A stuffed frog that had belonged to Grammy. Gramps won it at a carnival after successfully spearing three balloons. According to the tale that Grammy and Gramps loved to act out, he chose the frog from a whole slew of prizes because frogs grant wishes.

When he gave it to her, she was so delighted that she gave it a big old smooch then and there, looked at Gramps and said, "Wish granted." He'd asked her what she wished for, and she said, "A prince."

Yeah, I know. Corny. But I've clung to their story like a vine. Maybe something like their perfect love was out there for me, too.

Grammy gave me Igor when my dating prospects sucked as bad as a frog's choice of meal. And yep, Igor's magical abilities brought me and Jake together. The memory shot up like an unwelcome weed.

It'd been at a party my then-roommate and I hosted for the

Fourth of July, and Jake was brought along by our UPS delivery guy. (We'd invited our UPS delivery guy because he had great calves, and we figured he probably had friends with great calves. We were right.)

Igor was sitting on a table among my indoor plants because I thought he looked cute there, and Jake, at some point in the evening, asked me about him. I ended up explaining Igor's history, sure that a guy with great calves would smile awkwardly and hurry off.

Instead, he picked Igor up and held him at arms' length. Jake tilted his head and cocked a brow in an analytical-but-sexy kind of way. Toasty-brown eyes glimmering through wire-framed glasses. I'll never forget what he said.

"Looks like he's got one more prince in him."

Jake—the bastard—loved the fact that our relationship started all because of Igor, the carnival frog. He believed in the magic of perfect love just like I did.

But he stomped on that magic when he moved out and stole Igor. (Although he's denied it.) That's right. I've asked him. Politely. Calmly. *Diplomatically.* With every text and voicemail message I left, he replied that he didn't have Igor. But my frog was missing. The only plausible explanation was that Jake took him. But why? Why? To hurt me?

Straight up. I have some confidence issues. But that didn't mean I was on this frognapping mission because I believed Igor was what I needed to find love again. And it definitely wasn't because I secretly hoped Igor would reunite me and Jake.

Seriously. That's not what's going on.

Sasha from Balance, Bliss, Etc. said that sometimes taking matters into our own hands is the key to freeing our Inner Goddesses. So, I'm done being polite and calm and diplomatic. I will rescue Igor and end this doomed chapter of my life once and for all. I'm not just freeing my Inner Goddess. I'm raising her high above my head and waving her like a flag!

My search through the living room came up empty. I slunk into the hallway and saw three closed doors to the left. To the right, I saw beige countertops and a white fridge before the wall cut off the rest of the view. Doubtful Igor was in the kitchen, so I headed left.

I opened the first door. Bathroom. I was about to move on to the next room when I heard a key in the lock of the apartment door.

My heart seized. Full-on heart attack mode. Jake is back? Crap. Crap!

I jumped into the bathroom, barely taking the extra second to gently close the door behind me. My brain hummed with anxiety as I surveyed the limited options. Sink. Bathtub. Toilet. Another door. I turned the knob and peeked in. Linen closet. Stacked with shelves. No room for me.

Footsteps thudded down the hallway. My mouth went dry. I jumped into the tub, pulling the curtain closed, cringing as the metal hooks scraped along the shower rod. Glanced at my watch. What the hell? Barely nine o'clock. He must have forgotten something he needed for work. I held my breath and strained my ears.

Rustles and scratches sounded through the wall behind me. His bedroom? I didn't know the layout of the apartment, but it was the only thing that made sense. Please hurry and go, Jake.

Shit! I left the window in the living room wide-open. Shit. Shit. My armpits grew wet. If he catches me here, I'm so screwed. My heart slammed into my head. No way he'll believe I'm just looking for my frog. He already knows I can be…unhinged.

More noises through the wall behind me. What the hell was taking him so long? He should be at work, dammit.

The footsteps picked up again. Closer. Too close. Then the smooth turn of the doorknob.

Noooo. My stomach dropped. He was in the bathroom. The overhead light snapped on. Anxiety prickled along my hairline. The shower curtain wiggled. My eyes widened with horror as a hand reached in and turned on the faucet.

A spray of ice-cold water struck me full-blast in the chest. I gasped, raising my shoulders to my ears. His hand reached up to the shower head, adjusting the direction of the spray. Freezing water smacked my face. Spluttering, I raised my hands to fend off the attack of water. I clenched my shivering body, cursing my luck. Of course, unflappable Jake would believe in the health benefits of cold showers.

Over the blast of water, I could hear Jake singing and clothes falling to the floor. Shit. Ever so carefully, I scooched out of the icy stream, making my way to the opposite end of the tub, backing up against the faucet. Somehow, I had to get out—

The curtain shimmied. Jake was in the tub, beautifully naked.

His eyes found me. "*Ahhhh!*" He screamed like he discovered Norman Bates in his shower and grabbed the plastic curtain liner, holding it between us like a shield.

"Fee, Jesus Christ! What the hell are you—what the—"

The water pounded between us, and I was pretty sure I looked like some pitiful, unidentifiable creature washed up by the tide. Belatedly, I squeezed my eyes tight and spun to face the taps.

"I'm sorry! I'm sorry, oh my God, this wasn't how it was supposed to go."

Behind me, I heard him swearing as he jumped out of the tub. Telltale sounds of a towel. More swearing. Miserably, I killed the water and leaned my forehead against the chilly wall. This was so bad. So bad.

"Get out of there. Now," he commanded.

I blew out a breath as I searched for justifiable or forgivable explanations. Nothing jumped out at me.

Slowly, I pulled back the curtain with a trembling hand. I could barely meet his eyes, sizzling like browned butter. My wet sneakers squelched with each step.

Jake thrust a cotton towel at me. "Here."

"Thanks," I whispered, clutching it beneath my chin. He stood before me, clad waist-down in a towel. Fists on hips. I swallowed, willing my eyes to get back to his chiseled face, despite the snarl.

"You have thirty seconds to tell me why the hell you're trespassing my apartment before I call the police."

I half-expected the threat. It was so Jake. The guy had problems finding the funny, but I'd checked the "sense of humor" box regardless—so sure he'd lighten up eventually.

And me being me, I went on the offensive. "I'm sure the cops would love a break in their standard boring Tuesday morning." I viciously rubbed my arms with the towel. "Wonder what will interest them more. A woman hiding in a man's shower, or a man stealing a woman's frog."

Jake quirked an eyebrow. Okay. That sounded a lot more dramatic in my head.

"You can't be serious," he said.

"I just want Igor. Then I'm outta here. You'll never have to see me again."

"I didn't steal your frog. I've told you that a hundred times."

"Well, maybe you took him by accident. You blew out of our place so fast you'd think it was about to explode or something."

He looked away. "I don't have that stupid thing."

Ouch. The venom in his words stung my throat. Was I the only one who remembered what Igor meant to us?

"I don't appreciate the intimation that you didn't love him."

Jake scoffed, still avoiding my eyes. "Because it mattered to you, Fee. I've moved on. You should, too."

I read between the lines, my jaw dropping. "You're so full of yourself. I don't want him back because of what he meant to us or what he represented—"

"Clearly." Jake spread his arms to indicate our, or rather, my, humiliating situation.

My face heated. *Divert!* My eyes jumped around the room, gratefully landing on the pile of his clothing. Running shorts and sweat-dampened T-shirt. *Running?*

I pointed accusingly at his clothing. "Why aren't you at work, anyway? And who the hell has your precious Audi?" The words were deadly fast, spewing from my mouth before I had a chance to really think them through.

He finally met my eyes, and something flared in his gaze. Something intense. He clenched his jaw, and I didn't know if he was going to yell at me or pull me into his arms.

"Jake—"

He spun away. Left the bathroom. I stood frozen in place, shivering in my drenched clothes, wanting to be angry with him but finding anger with myself instead. Who the hell did I think I was, grilling him like his life was my business? I could practically hear my Inner Goddess chiding me right now. *Why am I such a natural at making everything worse? When will I learn?*

A flash of his face in the open doorway. "Let's go." Disappeared again. His frosty tone reminded me that he'd threatened to call the cops. Had I committed a jail-worthy crime? *Dumbass, of course you did. You broke and entered your ex's place. And your history doesn't help your situation.*

I ran my hands through my sopping hair. *Shit. I'm gonna have to ask Dad to bail me out.*

Again.

Closing my eyes briefly, I surrendered to my fate and left the bathroom. The last time I'd been in jail was for vandalism of public property. Six years ago. Marky-Mark, my then-boyfriend at the time, was part of a gang of taggers who was in a one-upmanship with other gangs.

He told me it'd be a fun and exciting night of creative expression.

Dad bailed me out. Forced me to dump Marky-Mark and agree to one-hundred hours of community service, otherwise he would take his name off my car loan. *That* episode was on the heels of *another* episode in which I got nabbed for pickpocketing with the "Italian Stallion," my boyfriend, in Milan.

Just to be clear—I hadn't actually succeeded in the final stage of the pickpocketing escapade. So, technically, my crime was really just feeling up an old lady. Stallion was the one who'd picked three wallets before a cop busted him.

Stallion took off, leaving me high and dry. But because I was clean, they couldn't hold me.

To make things even more humiliating, Stallion had apparently picked my pockets, too. So, I wasn't just clean. I was stranded. No passport. No ID. No money. No phone.

Dad told me that wasn't how he pictured his dream trip to Italy. Not sure which is more embarrassing now I'm thinking constructively about it. That I was still hooking up with loser guys in my thirties, or that I was still heavily reliant on my parents.

But I changed with Jake. Didn't I?

Jake led me into the room next to the bathroom—his bedroom. I wasn't there two seconds before he held out dry clothes to me. I almost accepted them, but then the unmistakable strap of a lacy, turquoise bra peeking out from within the stack of clothes halted my hand in mid-air. My stomach pitched.

Oh for God's sake.

He had a girlfriend.

And he was giving me her clothes.

No way in hell I'd put any of that on my body. I stepped back, folding my arms around my freezing-cold torso. "No thanks. Just give me Igor, and I'll skedaddle."

"Fee. Put on the damn clothes. I'll make you a cup of coffee."

"I don't want coffee. I want my frog."

Jake didn't respond. He threw on a T-shirt of his own, dropped his towel to finish dressing. I turned away as embarrassment set fire to my face and fixed my eyes on the view of the city outside his window.

"Meet you in the kitchen," he said. The click of the door signaled his exit, and my breath shuddered through closed lips.

I stared with a combination of confusion and sadness at his girlfriend's clothes waiting for me on the bed. He'd said he moved on, but I didn't think he meant it that way.

I sank onto the bed, clutching my hand to my chest. The pain in my heart was immeasurable. Worse than that moment when he left me. I can't believe I didn't see the signs, but now it was all so mortifyingly clear. Why he grew distant. Why he moved out with no warning. Oh God. His girlfriend must have his Audi.

Somewhere along the way, I must have messed up. Maybe I was too much of a free spirit. Maybe I was too much work. Maybe I was too much of a head-case.

So he hooks up with another woman? A woman who wears frilly lingerie, I thought with a huff and flicked the bra strap. How did they meet? Did she work with him? Suddenly, I was picturing them on the round table in the law firm's conference room. Gag.

Jake didn't just dump me. He let another woman come between us. How dare he—after all his promises, after all our sacrifices and compromises. My perfect, put-together Jake was a liar and a cheater. I can't believe I was stupid enough to fall for another jerk. What the hell was wrong with me?

Another thought pulled into the crowded parking lot of my overwhelmed brain. Clothes and coffee—did that mean he wasn't calling the cops? Ugh. Probably an empty threat. So, what was he planning instead? Sweet-talk his way through an explanation of why he cheated and lied? I scrubbed my hair with the towel as it dawned on me that he'd left me alone in his bedroom. *Dumb move, Jake Mackenzie.*

I ransacked the dresser and the closet. No Igor. Crouched on my hands and knees to scour under his bed when I caught a glimpse of myself in the full-length mirror nailed to the closet door. Shit, I was a sight. Crouched on the floor like some kind of drug addict searching for the last half-crushed pill under the bed. Blonde hair in need of a dye job limply hanging around my shoulders. The polar plunge I'd been subjected to did nothing for my makeup—streaky foundation, raccoon eyes.

Energy drained from my body. My butt sank to the floor, and I leaned against the bed. My eyes held the other pair of eyes in the mirror. A stranger stared back.

What the hell was I doing?

Proving to Jake he'd made the right call by walking away— that's what. When the chips are down, I go sideways. Here I am again, making things worse.

And looking pathetic doing it.

How in the world did I ever think any of this was a good idea? A B&E? Seriously? This was the kind of hot-mess thing I did pre-Jake. The kind of thing I promised I would quit doing. I'd promised Mom and Dad. I'd promised Sasha.

But did you promise yourself?

The voice came from the mirror. The somber question matched the sorry visage glaring back at me. I never promised myself because in the past, this kind of stupid stunt got me things I thought I wanted. Usually hot guys.

Face it, Fiona. It doesn't really matter anymore if Jake has Igor or not. It's no longer about Igor. Hell, maybe it never was about Igor. In a way, I'd hoped Jake took Igor because that would have meant he was hanging on to a part of our relationship. And I would have forgiven him!

But what does that say about me? Nothing good. It hurts and it sucks, but I can't keep throwing myself at him like this. He's moved on, and I've got to get control of my life.

Not quite sure what that meant, other than I knew I didn't like anything about me right then.

I got to my feet, shoes and socks now clammy warm, and left the room, his girlfriend's clothing mocking me from the bed.

At the entrance to the living room, I paused. My shame urged me to sneak out through the same window I arrived, pretend like none of this happened. My eyes lingered on the plants soaking in the newfound bright light.

Squaring my shoulders, I turned down the hallway toward the kitchen where the heavenly aroma of French roast beckoned.

I saw more than I wanted to as I entered the kitchen. Jake. Sitting at the café table by the window. Cup of coffee between his hands. An empty cup waited on the counter by the pot of coffee.

He didn't look up as I blew past.

Didn't say a word as I opened the door and closed it behind me.

THE BREEZE WAS cool for July, but it felt good after working in the yard all day. I smacked the excess soil from my hands as I surveyed the garden. A few days ago, my landlady's gardener had quit, leaving her in the lurch. I offered to help her out until she found another company to take over. She liked my work so much she offered me a full-time job landscaping not just this property, but all seven of her properties.

I still didn't know if I was more shocked that she saw a talent in me, or that she's paying me four times more than what I was already making.

A surge of accomplishment filled me as I admired the colors and textures playing against each other. I did this. Even though I had a terrible habit of screwing up my life, I did pretty okay with plants. My heart lifted. Know what? After I finish with the garden, I'm going to redecorate the—*my*—apartment. It was time.

I pressed the green button on the remote control for the garden fountain. A few choking sputters before a fine geyser of water erupted from the fountain's mouth. Yes! I gingerly stepped into the garden bed, placing my bare feet, one after the other, on the paver stones that wound a path between roses, gerbera daisies, coneflowers, and azaleas. The breeze came through, blowing the water as it arced from the sculpture. Mist sprayed my body. I whirled and whirled, letting the water hit me all over.

I was really enjoying this landscaping job, and who knows? Maybe someday I could start my own business. Get a whole bunch of clients. I mean, the graphic design freelancing was fine, but the work was inconsistent, short-term, and sporadic. All adjectives that earmarked my life—no, no, no—that earmarked my past. (My Inner Goddess was beaming right now.)

A car turned into the driveway of the triplex. My eyes bounced from the dull rims to the figure behind the wheel. Jake? My pulse skipped.

The engine cut off, and I swallowed as the driver's door opened. He's driving a Ford? Jake walked across the front yard, carrying a medium-sized cardboard box in both hands.

"You were drenched the last time I saw you, too, if I recall correctly," he said with a timid smile.

Oh. I looked around, suddenly coming to. I was standing statue-still in the stream of water spewing from the garden fountain's stone lips.

"Did you just crack a joke?" I asked, coming out of the garden and wringing the hem of my T-shirt.

"Too many late nights alone with SNL reruns and cheese popcorn."

That was a bullshit line. Eight days might have passed, but the memory of his girlfriend's lingerie was still emblazoned on my brain. I folded my arms. "What do you want, Jake?"

Nervousness scurried across his brows before he stepped forward and set the box on the ground.

"I came to apologize. I screwed up, Fee."

My arms tightened in wariness. "What's going on?"

"The first few times you accused me of taking Igor, I thought —" His face turned rose-red. "I thought it was an excuse to see me again."

My stomach clenched, and I struggled to keep my features poker-straight even though he'd seen a flash of my cards.

"But after the other week—" He took a deep breath. I'd never seen him this nervous before, not even when he was gearing up for the Wilson case. "I got to thinking it wasn't a lie. You really had lost him." He paused and then, with his left foot, nudged the box toward me.

Cautiously, I crossed the yard and crouched by the box. His unusual agitation and his apology sent my heart pounding. I opened the flaps.

There, right on top, was Igor.

"I didn't lose him," I snapped as I yanked Igor out of the box and clutched him like a long-lost child. "You stole him. You had him all along and made me scrounge around for him like some kind of—" My words cut short as my eyes lit upon the items that Igor had been resting upon.

I started pawing through framed photos, battered Sidney Sheldon paperbacks, and some clothes. *Wait a second.* Those were my photos and my books and my clothes. Why did he have all these things? I dug farther until my fingers stilled on turquoise lace.

What the hell was he doing? Giving me his girlfriend's clothes? I almost lifted the box to throw it at him, but the collection of items, everything piled together in this one box, told me I had everything wrong.

I blinked and shook my head, trying to clear out the buzzing confusion. Slowly, I pulled out the lacy turquoise bra. The bra he'd offered me last week.

My bra.

Holy shit. I totally forgot. We'd gone to Aruba for vacation, and the airline had lost my luggage. Of course, typical-me handled the inconvenience as though a tsunami had wiped out everything I owned. But Jake came through like the composed champ that he was. Found a local shopping mall and bought me a whole week's worth of clothing. He got my sizes and style right down to the exact detail—with a couple of his own preferences added in for flavor.

Like the lacy turquoise lingerie.

"This is—mine." My mouth was gummy. I sank to the grass. "I thought you were giving me another woman's clothes to wear." My brain felt as uselessly filled with cotton as Igor's. "I'm so lost. How come you have all this stuff?" I raised my eyes to his, shocked to find pure regret.

Jake sat in the grass across from me. "I didn't make partner, Fee." He yanked up a strand of grass and began to tear it apart. "And they let me go. And I couldn't—couldn't tell you. I was too ashamed."

Oh my God. That damn firm. Nothing more than a bunch of wrinkled old frat boys voting you in or voting you out, shuffling their eager protegés around like chess pieces. God, all those years he put in, climbing the ladder. He'd gotten so damn close, too, so close that he promised me a house on Lakeview Boulevard.

Then it hit me. This wasn't about another woman after all. I took in the Ford behind him. Less expensive than an Audi. Remembered he'd been running mid-morning, and now he was here, visiting me early afternoon. Was he still unemployed? I almost blurted out that he could have gotten another job, but I knew it was much more than that. He'd worked like a dog to become the perfect North, Vance, and Adams partner. Without the promotion, he probably thought he was nothing.

My chest tightened. I knew that nothing-feeling intimately.

"I'm so sorry. When did it happen?" I asked.

"Last week of April."

My jaw lowered, but words were slow to come. That's when he left me. My eyes roved the items in the box once again. "You lost your job, so you moved out." I shook my lacy bra in the air. "And stole my lingerie and Igor and my favorite books? Have you lost your flipping mind?"

Jake choked out a weak laugh. "Not exactly. Well, yeah, I probably lost my flipping mind, but I didn't steal—" He cleared his throat. "Look, I was a wreck. The only thing that made sense was to leave. It's stupid, I know. I just—I just couldn't face you and admit that I'd failed."

"You had Igor all along," I said, still not getting it. "You told me you didn't have him."

"I didn't know I had him," Jake said, stressing each word. "I found him last night." He exhaled and knuckled his hands through his hair. "When I made the decision to move out, I knew I had to do it before you got home. Otherwise, I'd choke." He wagged his head. "I was in a rush and grabbed stuff that I was sure was mine. Turned out, one of the boxes had some of your things mixed in." His face was now the color of the Rosa Black Baccara in the garden. "When I found your stuff with mine, it wrecked me. I couldn't keep unpacking. Just looking at your— your clothes," he said, stammering, "made me feel sick."

"Sick?" I reared back, shoulders stiff. "Wow."

"No. Not sick like that. Sick at myself," he said, hitting his chest. "Seeing your stuff made me feel sick because I'd screwed up a really great thing with you. But every time I thought about talking to you, telling you that I failed, that I was so messed up in the head that I accidentally took some of your stuff when I moved—I couldn't do it."

"Because you thought I'd be ashamed of you?"

He lowered his head. "I know how stupid it sounds. But yeah."

I stared at the box, unable to decipher the swirling in my gut. He never called, never texted to let me know he'd found some of my things. Just—stayed away from me.

"All this time, I thought it was me." I looked up at the sky. "You realize that's why I got a little loony."

"Yeah. But—I think that reassured me in a weird way." He spread out his hands. "Igor kept you coming back. He was the reason I'd get a call from you or whatever. And I think, on a subconscious level, I didn't want that to stop." He gnawed on his lower lip. "I told myself I didn't have him, but I also didn't try too hard to prove that to you, because if I found him or didn't find him, that'd be it. You'd stop coming around."

How ironic. My obsessive behavior kept us connected. Hmm.

"I finally realized that after the other day. So I went through everything I put in storage. Igor was at the bottom of one of the boxes. Wrapped in a bag. Totally missed him. I'm sorry."

I waved my fingers over sprouted dandelions. It wasn't me. I wasn't the problem. But I'd invented thirty-eight reasons to explain why I'd chased him off.

"You called Igor stupid," I mumbled.

"I didn't mean it. I was—you caught me off-guard. I wasn't ready to explain about my job, about what a failure I am." Silence lasted for the length of two irregular heartbeats. "Fee, I love Igor. And I love you."

The implications of what he was saying rang through my head like a hi-striker at a carnival. My heart stuttered as those golden-brown eyes locked onto mine. I broke our staring contest to watch a bird play in the bath.

My hands squeezed Igor. I trained my focus on the rainbow shimmering in the arc of water. Jake said the things I've been wanting him to say ever since he walked out. This was what I wanted. Igor brought him back. Igor helped me find love again. This frog really did grant wishes.

"I can't, Jake. I'm sorry."

Finally, I looked at him. That gorgeous face. That body. His nearness was almost enough to send my heart into overdrive. *Almost.*

"It's true I wanted you back." I wiggled Igor's head. "He was a handy excuse, you're right. But I got a good dose of medicine that day. There I was, crawling around your floor like some miserable waste—" I sighed. "If I can't be okay as me, just me, then I'm not okay. You know?"

He pursed his lips. "Yeah. I know." Birds swooped overhead, playing tag through the spray of water. We shared a sad smile before he slowly got to his feet. He held out his hand, and for one last time, I let him help me stand.

SYLVIA AND JACK
REGINA SOKAS

Seven-sisters coed Sylvia Plath contemplates taking a walk on the wild side after meeting an older, bohemian, rogue named Jack Kerouac.

Regina Sokas has published straight-news, feature articles, poetry, and short stories. Her advertising copy was quoted on the front page of The Wall Street Journal. She has two completed novels currently in search of a home.

PLAYLIST

That Doggie in the Window — **Patti Page**
I'm Walking Behind — **Eddie Fisher**
Rags to Riches — **Tony Bennett & Elton John**
The Song from Moulin Rouge — **Connie Francis**
Mama He Treats Your Daughter Mean — **Ruth Brown**

Scan to listen at buttonhall.com/books/left-turns

Miss Sylvia Plath added another teaspoon of sugar to her mug. She'd had to settle for coffee as tea was not on offer. She found sugar sometimes calmed the mind, although it shouldn't. At least, that's what her mother had taught her, quoting a highly regarded nutritionist who once taught at Goucher. Or was it Vassar? She caught herself moving the spoon with too much vigor so that it bounced against the mug's thick ceramic sides. It would have been an appalling noise, if one had been able to hear it over the din of neighboring voices.

These weren't her usual haunts, this subterranean spot in the thick of Bohemia, Greenwich Village. The walls of the basement establishment were brick and there appeared to be soot on them. She had visited a darling little bookstore just blocks away, the kind with nooks and crannies hiding treasures along winding paths, and, after diligent browsing, had decided that she and her new purchase could use a cup of tea. Ah, well. As for being this far South in the city, her anxiety sometimes had a way of taking her off on long walks and, anyway, why was she justifying herself to herself? When did she become her own nanny? Too many rules had been imprinted on her, she feared, for her to ever become a great poet.

In fairness to the boisterous party disrupting her reading, the brick walls and tin ceiling did little to absorb sound. No carpeting, unless you counted the thick litter of discarded peanut shells. Still, the ever-expanding crowd at the next table made no effort to modulate their voices. They rasped and roared and roiled with laughter as though the world was built for their comfort. Dragging chairs from all corners of the room, they swelled against the confines of brick and tin, invading the spaces around them thoughtlessly, small children with toy drums. Sylvia had never been gifted a toy drum as a child. It was too late to take up such foolishness now.

She shook her head at the fanciful thought and attempted to return her attention to her book.

"Jack! It's Jack!" a man cried out with such joy that Sylvia felt compelled to glance up. Her view was blocked by a woman who had leapt to her feet.

"You aren't using this, are you?" The woman with a ragged pixie of a haircut commandeered Sylvia's spare chair without even pretending to wait for permission. It was true, though, that she was not expecting anyone to join her. No one knew where she was. She'd slipped away. Slipping away. It sounded like a little death. Something one might do in the bath.

The boy who overtook Sylvia's once-spare chair looked nothing like death. There was something athletic in his ease of movement, in the breadth of his shoulders and the set of his jaw... some confidence that spoke of crisp Autumn weather, the flurry of leaves, the cheers of the crowd.

Suddenly their eyes met, hers and the boy - no surely a man - named Jack. He grinned. Caught in her intrusion, Sylvia quickly looked away. Eyes locked on the book she could no longer read, she fancied she could feel his gaze still. Only when she sensed he had settled at the table, heard him speaking to the others, only then did she recognize that she had been holding her breath and released it with a soft sigh.

It was a long-standing habit of hers, spinning fancies on the lives of strangers, investing them with history and character and motive. A harmless habit, she thought, and safer with strangers. She had been burnt to the soul from spinning fantasies about the character and motive of people who actually moved in her own orbit. They were far too prone to break the gravitational pull of her imagination, and collision was inevitable. She carried the craters in her psyche.

Another roar of laughter from the next table sliced through her inward state, brought her crashing back into the room. Involuntarily, she glanced at them, only to find the man named Jack staring directly into her eyes. They linked. Connected. Froze in a strange sort of intimacy that stilled the chaos. Then he winked at her.

Spell broken. Deeply embarrassed, a flushing Sylva gathered up her things and fled to the safety of the street.

The footsteps rushing up behind her were muffled by the shouts and horns and cacophony that colored New York streets, so when he tapped her on her shoulder the touch sent her spinning. She would have fallen, had the man named Jack not taken her by the arm and steadied her. Their eyes met again. His were laughing.

Sylvia was not the sort of girl men chased down the street. Oh, she knew she wasn't ugly, but being recently described by a fashion editor as having a "coltish charm" only emphasized her gangly figure. Of course, Sylvia knew that colts grew into horses and feared she was in danger of aging into one of those horse-faced women with stern looks. She wished she knew how to spontaneously laugh along with him, but the moment passed.

"May I?" Jack said, but he was already reaching for the book she clutched to her chest. He slipped it from her numb fingers.

Pulling out a pen, he flipped the book open. "Mildred?" Doubt and humor in the single word. The book was clearly second hand, the inscription in the front penned in a flowery, old-fashioned-looking script. He was playing with her.

"Don't I look a Mildred?" Sylvia surprised herself by matching his tone.

"No. No, you don't." He studied her slowly. "Something softer. Something that flows, no, floats on the breath like a sigh in the night. Something that sneaks up on a man."

Her mouth was dry, but she managed. "Sylvia. My name is Sylvia."

"That's it. Of course. Perfect. Sylvia. Sylvie," he purred the last in a credible French accent. "Spirit of the wood. Goddess of the forest. She who lives in the trees that become the very books we love to hold."

With that, he quickly wrote in the book, snapped it shut, and handed it back to her. "It's been a pleasure." With a wink and a grin, he was gone.

After she watched him head back to his friends, that athletic lope still there, she opened the book and read, "My mysterious Sylvie, Call me." A phone number was followed by a signature that was all angles and slopes as if it threatened to tumble down the page. Jack Kerouac.

It was lucky for him, she thought, attempting to regain her composure, that this wasn't a precious book, wasn't, for example, her Dylan Thomas poems. Defacing that would have been unforgivable.

SHE HAD no intention of ever calling him, but the summer had been difficult. Sylvia was lonely among the girls attending the prestigious internship alongside her. Their interests were more, well, cozy. Not to say that the other girls were wrong. If cozy were a realistic objective, wouldn't that be enough? After all, the magazine promoted a lifestyle comfortable with kitten heels and Peter Pan collars. It was simply that Sylvia had left her childhood behind at the age of eight. Even little, she had never been at home in an atmosphere redolent of kittens and Peter Pan.

The Plath household was not a kittenish fairy tale. Life was difficult and unfair. You could first be condemned by blood, for she had heard her father railing against the prejudices stirred by war against a man, no matter his many talents, who spoke with the accent of the enemy. Then you could be killed by blood. One bad toe, and his blood carried the poison up through his body and deadened him for good. Her father's death had been both tragic and ridiculous.

In any event, restless one evening, she dialed the number. It was answered by a man who laughed when she asked for Jack.

"Has our boy bagged another quail? Well, then, my little bird, you are welcome to come tonight. He will be here."

Caught without paper and pen, she memorized the address.

SYLVIA HAD DRESSED CAREFULLY but had achieved a look that was neither chic nor bohemian, just pedestrian. Scanning the room for Jack, she saw a motley assortment of people already in various stages of inebriation perched on unsuitable seating surfaces: a massive desk, an upturned crate, and the floor. Mostly the floor. In the center of one group sat the largest ashtray Sylvia had ever seen. It overflowed with ash and butts.

And suddenly there was Jack. "It's you. I had hoped it was you. Sylvan Sylvia, Goddess of the Woods."

Sober Sylvia wondered who else it might have been, how many possibilities, strange women to whom had he passed his telephone number. There was another, Silly Sylvia, who wanted to believe that a strange man who chased her down the street did so in the throes of an irresistible love at first sight.

Still, she fantasized about being in a place where nobody she knew could ever come, where she could be anonymous. She had achieved that.

"Do you often throw such big parties on weekdays?" The minute the question left her lips, Sylvia wished that she could reel it back in. She sounded like her mother.

"Ha! It's not my party. The guest of honor here is that bearded ruffian over there, our visiting man of letters returned from San Francisco for the week, young Allen Ginsberg."

Sylvia saw a bespeckled young man with unruly hair. Jack pulled her over to a different group. He accosted a woman with a long, brown, braid trailing down her back. "Desi, pour my girl Sylvia here a drink."

The woman pressed her lips with displeasure, but handed Sylvia a chipped mug that looked as if it could have been stolen from the café where she first saw Jack just a few days ago. Sylvis took a healthy sip and began to cough.

"Looks like you have an amateur here, Jack. You aren't robbing the cradle, are you?"

"I'm in college," Sylvia protested.

"A co-ed. Buttercup, if you're hoping for a sloe gin fizz or a grasshopper, you've wandered into the wrong establishment. We don't stock little paper umbrellas here, either," the woman said with a cruel grin.

Just the other day, Sylvia thought she had finally found her drink. Vodka. She had embraced the sharp, swift, cleaving as the tasteless beverage invaded her body, severing feeling from thought. This brown liquid took a detour, landing in her head and not her stomach. No power. No godliness. No finesse. A ham-fisted invasion. She shivered.

"Don't mind Desi. Bitterness is her artform." Jack took Sylvia by her free hand and led her through the crowd to an alcove. There five or six people sat cross-legged or sprawling on a mattress that lay bed-less on the floor.

Sylvia sat silently sipping on her whisky, her throat growing more welcoming to the liquid warmth, bringing her inside to match the exterior. The crowded apartment was over-warm on the summer night, the open windows doing little but swapping hot city street air for smoky hot cigarette-speckled air. The conversation swirling around her was of unfamiliar names and places. She had nothing to add.

Jack didn't bother with introductions. She was 'anonymous

girl'. No one here, but for Jack, knew her name. That pleased her, and she took a bigger sip. Then one of the men produced a small, flat, oddly shaped, clay pipe. He produced a bit of foil which contained a miniature black brick. Pinching off a piece, he rolled it into a little ball perhaps smaller than a pea and placed the ball into the pipe's tiny bowl.

The man looked at Jack with an eager expression. "You'll appreciate this stuff, Jack. Opiated hashish. Newly arrived in New York."

"Fire it up," Jack said.

The pipe made its rounds. Sylvia struggled a bit, getting the hang of holding the tiny clay pipe. She almost singed her hair when it slid forward toward her face as she bent over the pipe, sucking at the flame.

The hashish man burbled to Jack like a fan. "*The Town and the City* was magnificent. I couldn't believe that someone I knew was that genius. Everything is collapsing, so pass the pipe! When will we get the next one, Jack?"

"It's done, my best work yet. Like Monk and Parker spin the notes, man, I've brought the spontaneity of bop to words. Words poured out. Scrolled out. It should be published on a scroll, but publishers today have no imagination. They want the world to be safe. The only truth is music. My words are music. It has to have the beat. Move propulsively. I have to be in motion."

Jack was a writer, then. Not just a writer, but the author of a book someone had seen fit to publish. Sylvia felt that she ought to have known that, but her embarrassment drifted off with the intoxicating smoke she exhaled.

Jack laughed now. "Listen to me. Me. Me. Self is an illusion..."

Jack's voice became entwined with that smoke that rose up from the bed as the tiny pipe continued its rounds. Sylvia slipped in and out of listening. At one point, when she rejoined the group for a moment, she noted that the conversation had descended into dirty jokes. There was talk of breasts. She chose to tune back out and floated on the unfamiliar hashish into the depths of her own mind.

OTTO CAME TO HER THEN. Daddy. Borne on a cloud of his beloved bees, his missing leg fully restored, his missing life fully restored. But they were meeting now as strangers. Some primitive, pagan hand had drawn a thick curtain against the girl who had existed before Daddy's death.

"Why do you come here?" she whispered to the specter. "Too late. Too late. My childhood has crumbled into dust, beautiful, inaccessible, obsolete dust."

He just looked at her, stern as a rock.

"She who was is now gone," Sylvia cried. It was not a lie, or at least not a deliberate one. No matter how strong her daytime determination to make her mark in society, the Sylvia who dreamt at night honored no checkpoints or border stations. That Sylvia roamed at will, consorting with whomever she pleased, even if it was Death in a fine suit.

Not that Death shunned the sunlight. He was always dependable.

Not like the father who died when she was just eight years old, who only haunted her when she was wide awake. Just a shadow. He left her the same year that she had her first poem published in *The Boston Herald*. How, suddenly, had he changed his schedule to show himself so plainly tonight? He shook his head sternly at her. She was bathed in blame. Was her ambition deadly? How many would it kill?

Otto appeared healthy. (She called him Otto now, even in her sleep, the word Daddy too painful to endure. Though never to his face, of course. Never to his face. Outrageous to even think it.) His lips moved, but it was difficult to hear him over the buzzing of the bees. So many bees. An army of bees, it would take untold numbers to so successfully drown out the thunder of his voice. No words, and yet some wave of sound washed over her. Knocking her off her stride. "Don't be angry," she whimpered.

Then she felt arms wrapping around her, pulling her into a broad chest. Oh, how she had longed for Daddy to hold her as he must have before. Didn't he? She fell into the warmth of the time before, and the arms enveloped her.

Just as she felt herself unwrapping her shroud to emerge into this warmth, lips began nibbling on her neck. The incongruity pierced the shadows of sleep, jolting her back into the party room.

Startled, she jabbed a sharp elbow to free herself.

"Ow," Jack said. "Are you always so violent or did I catch you on a bad trip?"

Violent? She wasn't the one sneaking up on people wielding lips. She pulled away from him. "Was I dreaming then? Or am I dreaming now?"

"Ah, don't be embarrassed that you fell asleep. We can be a dull, old crowd some nights." He made no mention of the liquor or the hashish, both of which played their part in muddling her head.

Indignant. How dare he assume to assign her an emotional state. Defensive. "I'm not –"

"I once fell asleep of an evening," he interrupted her as if she had not spoken at all, "and when I woke up in a strange hotel room, I had completely forgotten who I was. I really didn't know who I was at all for a good fifteen seconds. Seconds sounds like a short time, but fifteen seconds..."

He reached for her hand, and slowly unfurled her fingers. "One," he said, kissing a single finger. "Two." And the next finger. And so on for all five fingers and six now for the palm. Wrist next, outside and in, tickling her pulse with a nibble. Elbow, inside. His breath raced along her vein. And elbow outside. Jack had counted to ten now, each kiss lingering on her skin for the full second. Eleven, the shoulder. That, at least, was protected by her shirt, giving her a heartbeat of recovery. Twelve, with one finger he slid open her top button and found her collarbone.

Sylvia held her breath, mind racing ahead to number 15, as he progressed from collarbone to the side of her jaw, her chin, and, when on fifteen his lips met hers, she fell into the kiss as if the portal to that lost childhood world of magic had somehow opened wide again.

When he started to pull away, she threaded her fingers through his dark curls and pulled him in. She thought that if they stopped too soon, she might just start to cry. She didn't know why but believed that the tears would fly from her eyes, sobs from her throat, and she might not be able to stop for days and days and days.

Her desperation must have tasted like passion because when they finally pulled apart Jack looked exceedingly pleased with himself. Coming into her senses, Sylvia realized that she was still on the dirty mattress, still surrounded by others, some of whom were now sniggering. Muttering excuses, she fled to the bathroom.

While she was washing her face in the bathroom, the woman Desi burst through the unlockable door. Without a sign of hesitation, Desi pulled down her trousers and sat on the toilet.

"There's just one bathroom, you know. Other people have needs, too." Desi threw Sylvia a disgusted look.

Sylvia caught her breath.

Desi eyed her with something like contemptuous sympathy. "Look, I don't know what he's done – and I don't want to know.

Keep your sorry little story to yourself. Jack has no real, beating, heart for anyone but himself. Not his wife. Not his baby girl. Not a blonde coed hiding in the only bathroom."

A wife? A baby girl? Sylvia began soaping her hands with real vigor, as if Lady MacBeth had entered her body.

She felt very still and empty, the way the eye of a tornado must feel, moving dully along in the middle of the surrounding hullabaloo. From a dark corner of the room, Sylvia stood watching Jack from the shadows, watching a new girl thrust her hips toward him, and imagined their tongues attacking one another as their mouths met. She could feel herself slowly being forgotten, drifting away like the smoke that still curled toward the ceiling before making its way to an open window.

"Don't let him fuck with your mind." Sylvia turned to the voice that belonged to Allen, the purported guest of honor.

"What?" The language was harsh. The message harsher.

"Our Jack. He has many talents. Fidelity is not one of them."

"He needn't be faithful to me. He barely knows me. I'm not his wife."

"That I already knew, having met both wife number one and wife number two. He hasn't landed on a number three yet."

Two already? Sylvia froze her face, determined not to look surprised. Or hurt. "It's nothing to me."

"What is nothing but a different kind of something? So, what is your passion, leaving Jack out of the equation?"

"What do you mean?"

"Surely there is one fire in you that burns hotter than the others. I have a deep curiosity about the spiritual realm, including the Buddhism that our boy Jack introduced me to on his way out that door. I have the human weakness of wanting to love and be loved. I cavort with the best minds of my generation. I flirt with madness – and it flirts back at me. Yet, through all of this, one thing stands out. I am a poet."

Swept along with the torrent, Sylvia responded, "I am, too." She sucked in her breath with surprise at the certainty of her tone.

"Published?"

"Yes."

"First publication?"

"*The Boston Herald*. Age eight."

"Prodigy. Mine was *The Morning Call*. Age eleven."

He began laughing then, a rich and complex sound coming from a deep place. A beautiful sound. Sylvia found herself laughing along with him, but then kept laughing until tears flew from her eyes, the laughter escaping from her throat like a sob. Hysteria was winking from the corner.

Allen made no move to hush her. That was the first inclination of most people, the there-there-now sort of do-shut-up. He simply stood there, a solid presence, waiting. At last, he said, "Poets are a little mad. Or maybe it isn't poets, but just me. Maybe I'm the only one nuts. The one thing I know is that I am nuts. The doctors tell me so."

This was more shocking than discarded wives, more shocking than hashish, this casually admitting to madness. This was more intimate than kisses. More intimate than what might have followed the kisses. "I am, too."

"So, you see then: poets are damned, but we see with the eyes of angels."

There seemed to be no point in lingering. What was meant to happen that night was now written in the book of life. When Sylvia left the party, she didn't bother trying to find the host or hostess to politely make her goodbyes. She didn't bother saying goodbye to Jack, either. She simply wrapped the mantle of a damned angel around her as protection against the world and stepped out into the street.

AUTHOR'S NOTES:

The phrase 'the best minds of my generation' is taken from Ginsberg's *Howl*. There is some internet disagreement about who said 'poets are damned, but we see with the eyes of angels,' Ginsberg or William Carlos Williams speaking about Howl.

The story of waking in the hotel room was adapted from Jack Kerouac's *On The Road*.

The phrase 'beautiful, inaccessible, obsolete' is taken from Sylvia Plath's *Johnny Panic and the Bible of Dreams*. The sentence '...felt very still and empty, the way the eye of a tornado must feel, moving dully along in the middle of the surrounding hullabaloo' is taken from *The Bell Jar*.

GARLIC AND BUTTER
SHERRILL NILSON

When Nancy finds a talking, cannibalistic snail in her jewelry box, her life quickly goes off the rails

---

Sherrill has been a lot of things—Parent, earth mother, environmentalist, cattle rancher, horse breeder, tarot card reader, late-life grad student, traveler to strange lands. She's lived in Tulsa and outside a small town in Oklahoma, in Ruidoso and Santa Fe, New Mexico, San Francisco, Austin, and back home to Tulsa. She published a sci-fi trilogy and is currently writing her fourth book.

PLAYLIST

Fly on the Wall — **Miley Cyrus**
People Are Strange — **The Doors**
Cannibals — **Mark Knopfler**

Scan to listen at buttonhall.com/books/left-turns

There was a snail in Nancy's jewelry box. Quite a large snail, too, sitting on her lapis lazuli pendant. What the hell is a snail doing in my jewelry box? How did he get here?

If one snail eats another snail—Nancy had read somewhere —he retains the memory of the snail he eats. "But," she wondered, "does he (How do I know this is a he?) retain his own memory, or does the horror of what he's done blot out all memory of the self who ate another snail?"

"Not at all," said the snail, startling Nancy more than a little, "And what horror are you thinking of? I get hungry. This is a nice piece of lapis lazuli you've got here," as he crawled, or snailed, across her necklace.

"His mouth isn't moving, and he can read my thoughts. I've been working too hard lately."

"It's not so surprising if you're logical about it," said the snail, ignoring Nancy's second startled jump. "If you will notice, I am a rather large snail for my kind, anyway."

He paused, and Nancy thought she imagined a sardonic smile. Could snails smile?

"I have, you see, developed a taste for other snails. Rather a good way to acquire knowledge, don't you think? Sometimes, I encourage the sweet young snails to read things I would like to know about and tell them what they should study to better themselves. They are the better for it, you know. Yes, snails smile. And you may be right. I have, perhaps, developed a certain cynicism. I shall have to watch that. What do you wear these pink enamel earrings with? They are certainly, umm, colorful." He was a tactful snail.

"Sweet young things?" Nancy wondered. What were the memories of sweet young things? Did snails go through puberty? She didn't need thoughts of adolescent snails cluttering her mind. Her own teenage memories were embarrassing enough.

"I am not a pervert. I do not eat children. Their minds do not have enough information yet to be valuable." He paused, thoughtfully cocking his head, "They are quite creative, though."

Noticing the still puzzled state of Nancy's mind, he continued patiently, "I encouraged several to study brains, and that, of course, led me to the study of thought. One particularly tasty young thing was quite brilliant and gave me a good amount of useful information about thought patterns and energy. Telepathy, you see."

"Did he eat his fellow snails cooked in garlic and butter?" Too late, she tried to suppress the thought.

"Please! What a horrid thought!" The snail withdrew into his shell for a moment. Then his head poked out, and Nancy caught a nasty gleam in his eye as he said, "But what could I expect from someone who eats cows and chickens and fat dull lumps of potatoes? I certainly cannot imagine gaining anything from filling yourself with the memories of some placid neutered bovine stuffed with corn, half of whose short life was spent standing in its own waste matter. And what could a potato have a memory of anyway? Earthworms and plastic bags and pimple-faced supermarket stock boys?"

"What I learn, I learn on my own. I don't have to be a cannibal to do it," said Nancy, aloud for the first time and rather startling herself.

The snail's antennae waved wildly.

"Of course, of course," smiled the snail, "But please, it isn't necessary to shout."

"I think I'm going crazy," muttered Nancy to herself. "Snails can't talk, and what is a snail doing in my jewelry box? Ugh! Slug!"

"There is no need for you to get huffy about it," said the snail, stung by Nancy's distaste for snails, at least without the benefit of garlic and butter. "I am not a slug. Snails are not slugs.

We are a fine and honorable species. Some of us have shells far more beautiful than what you have here in this box of, I must say, rather tacky trinkets."

"Honorable?" That raised Nancy's left eyebrow a little. Telling pretty little snails what to study to better themselves and then having them for dinner? She ignored his slur on her taste in jewelry. He was probably right anyway; she didn't have money for expensive jewelry.

"All in the pursuit of knowledge," huffed the snail. "What I am doing is quite important, quite important."

"Poking around in other people's minds," thought Nancy.

"In the first place, I am not 'people'; I am a snail. And in the second place, I am using a time-honored method of learning," he paused, then went on, "In the third place, can't you think of instances where you'd like to know what someone else is thinking? In the fourth place, how else could I communicate with you? In the fifth place, most people's minds are decidedly uninteresting."

That made Nancy think of Fred. He'd be here any minute to take her to dinner.

"Of course. I could teach you. It would be an interesting experiment. Though possibly only some rudimentary basics. It's all that cow you eat."

"What do you suggest I eat? Snails?" snapped Nancy.

The snail disappeared into his shell.

"I'm sorry," Nancy was immediately contrite. She was interested in knowing what Fred might be thinking. Though reading his mind might be an exercise in futility.

And this skill could come in handy at work, too. Very handy. As an attorney, it would be a great help to know what witnesses on the stand were thinking and what was going on in the opposing counsel's mind.

"Very well," said the snail. "Your dietary habits are natural to your species, if unfortunate. But you seem extraordinarily empathic for a human; perhaps you could learn. We'll try."

"Are all snails like you?" asked Nancy.

"Oh, no. I have my specialty; others have their specialties. This study is my unique area. And, I might add, not altogether approved of by my colleagues. That happens all too often when a scholar branches out into a new area of study. It takes some time for new ideas to be accepted, however useful and brilliant they may be."

Nancy smothered her thoughts about inflated male snail egos as quickly as she could, but the snail cocked his head at her suspiciously.

"I think," he turned toward a mother-of-pearl necklace, one of Nancy's favorite pieces of jewelry. "I would like this beautiful, polished shell to sit on while we begin—so cool and smooth. Let's go somewhere more comfortable, shall we? It's stuffy in your jewelry box. Not too near the heater, please, and out of the sun."

"That's the necklace I was going to wear," thought Nancy with some dismay.

"It's too gaudy for that pink sweater, much too large for you, and besides, you shouldn't wear shells in winter," he said as he primly adjusted himself in the center of the pearly shell. "Over there, I think."

"Pompous much?" Nancy carried the shell, snail ensconced, to the table beside the small stuffed chair in the corner of her bedroom he indicated.

"Clear your mess off this table, please, while I collect my thoughts about how we are to begin. I've never attempted anything like this before. If this works, I have much knowledge I could impart to you. You have a great deal of room in your mind. Virtually an empty slate. I'm quite excited."

She registered the insult, ignored it, picked up her coffee cup, a plate with muffin paper and crumbs on it, and headed to the kitchen, wondering if he could still hear her thoughts from there.

"Only the first part," he said when she returned. "As you move further away your thoughts become a part of the general hum and impossible to differentiate. About fifteen feet is the maximum, and then only when there are not too many others about. It can become all a jumble then, you see. Now, to begin."

"I suppose," said Nancy. She was not very sure about all this. Yes, he is an exceptional snail, but what would this do to her mind? She already felt she was going crazy. And she was a little concerned about the snail's motives.

"There is no need to be frightened. This is an important experiment for me. I recently ate an interesting cross-species communication student, and I'm here because I wished to try it out for myself. I shall begin by explaining the basics to you."

Nancy wondered how long this would leave her to get ready for her date with Fred.

"Don't worry, this first session will be quite brief. This will probably take several sessions, but time is relative, you know. Now, shall we proceed?"

Thirty minutes later, Nancy was brushing her teeth when the doorbell rang.

"Hey, Fred," she called, "Door's open. Come on in. I'm almost ready."

Fred looked around, sniffing the air. "Hey, darlin'," he called through the bathroom door, "I thought we were going for pizza? It smells like you've been cooking."

"God," he thought, "like she'd ever offer to cook for me. I get so tired of taking her out all the time. She eats like a horse and never offers to go Dutch, much less pay for anything. I gotta get rid of this girlfriend. There must be something better out there. Somebody not fat, maybe."

Nancy cleared her throat. She was standing in the doorway, much less than fifteen feet away.

"Oh, hi. Didn't see you standing there. You ready, or did you already eat? Smells like garlic in here."

Nancy didn't answer—just looked at him with narrowed eyes.

"What?... What?" said Fred.

WINGS

MELISSA HED

An otherworldly mother wrestles with the emotional trials of parenting.

Once upon a time, Melissa Fischler Hed was a litigator, but she grew tired of people arguing and sought a more fulfilling way to help people. Today, she works as a quantum energy healer, transitions coach, and soul midwife providing holistic end-of-life care. She's also a freelance writer and editor, Co-Director of the Squam Writes Retreat, and the former Managing Editor at Your Teen Media. You can read more about her at: melissahed.com

---

PLAYLIST

B-Side — **Khruangbin & Leon Bridges**
Godmother — **Noga Erez**
Creep — **Radiohead**
Blackbird — **The Beatles**
Lovely Day — **Bill Withers**

Scan to listen at buttonhall.com/books/left-turns

M other thought she knew how to calm Creature. Soothing voice. Gentle touch. Stalwart presence. Unwavering love. Mother tried all these techniques, and more.

Still, Creature cried. Then worse, when Mother tried to swaddle Creature in mullein leaves, their cries turned volcanic. Roaring with frustration, they wrestled off containment, then stomp-toddle-ran from Mother's reach with surprising speed.

Alarm pinged against the walls of Mother's heart like she'd been caught in a hunter's snare. When at last she found Creature lying on the ground beneath a canopy of sumac, she collapsed to her knees alongside them in supplication, wailing. "Please, please, tell me what you need!"

Creature answered by jabbing Mother's soft spots with their feet, knees, hands, arms, and elbows, conveying they did not want Mother around.

Instructor told Mother in times like these she should not abandon her sentry. Mother's job, her most important job, was to stay, be present, and bear witness. "All Creation wants someone who won't abandon them when they feel broken, and fix whatever's wrong. But what you can do and what you should do are not always in alignment. Sometimes it's best to bear witness as the weak and innocent learn to protect themselves from harm."

Mother could not imagine abandoning Creature. Were they hurting? Were they afraid? Did they realize she offered comfort and protection? Mother hovered like an osprey in a hailstorm protecting its one precious egg. If only Creature could explain what was wrong.

For Mother knew the terror of aloneness. She knew once terror took hold of you, it sank into your spirit and set up a home. The memory of standing alone in a crowd of angry humans, screaming for her mother till she was voiceless, never left her. She did not wish that same torment for Creature. She resolved to protect them from pain.

Before Creature came, Mother had so thoroughly researched various methods of successful rearing that she convinced herself she entered this arrangement fully prepared. Now though? She was unsure of herself and her learning.

Creature keened when Mother uttered soothing words. Rubbing circles on Creature's back made them shrink from her touch and scramble away.

Oh, how their wails tangled knots in Mother's hair and the thoughts inside her head! She could not think. She needed air. She needed quiet. She needed to rise and distance herself—just for a moment—to gather her wits and breathe.

Creature quieted at Mother's departure. They turned on their belly, starfished their arms and legs wide, and pressed their wet cheek to moss-covered earth. Then they drowsily closed their eyes.

Mother saw all this from the archway loosely woven by repeated passage through bramble bush whips, leaves, and thorns.

"Stay. Be present. Witness." Instructor's advice was sound, after all. Mother did not need to fix anything for Creature. She felt her nerves calm for an exquisite moment.

Then they hurled upward again and grew taut.

Creature was too quiet.

Were they breathing?

Mother scanned Creature's chest for the rise and fall.

There, there it was. Mother felt somewhat reassured now.

Creature took in a long breath, then smiled briefly as they lay sleeping. Were they dreaming? And, what sort of mother would be jealous of a dream that made Creature smile?

Mother realized for the first time and quite suddenly, she was not the cure-all, or even a balm for Creature's pain. She was not

—could not be—completely responsible for Creature's happiness. Creature was a part of her, certainly—but also, once animated, not entirely hers at all.

The revelation stunned her. Then loneliness took hold of her heart and dug in its claws.

THREE MORNINGS LATER, after gorging on wild grapes and chickweed, Creature climbed a rope tower and stayed there, at its pinnacle, limned in golden-white rays of the sun.

Below, Mother sat waiting on a bench in what the humans called a playground. She rolled sugar ants between her long slender fingers, then swallowed the misshapen balls whole. Sometimes an adult or a child dared sit next to her. Most of the time, her seatmates were birds. Doves, house wrens, blue jays, starlings, a crow, and even a red-breasted woodpecker stopped by to fluff out their feathers and preen. The birds didn't want the sugar ants she offered, so she fed them peanuts, sunflower seeds, and millet instead.

Morning shadows shrank at midday, then grew long again and faded in the gloaming. A woman or man (it was so difficult to discern between genders) wrestled a child into their jacket while its older sibling threw rocks at the bats swooping down to feed on mosquitoes, trying to knock them off course and down from the sky.

Adults spared not even a glance for her, nor for Creature, being so much more concerned with dumping sand from sneakers than the welfare of a stranger and a young one high up on the rope tower all alone.

By the time the spiny tips of shoulder blades poked through Creature's back, all the humans had long departed.

"It hurts," Creature said.

"I remember," Mother answered, for those were also the first words Mother spoke when she came into this world.

She distracted Creature, first by telling them to watch the sunset, then by teaching them to answer, "It's me-me-me. I'm here-here-here," to the Great Horned owl's call.

After a while, Creature's head drooped and their vocal cords wheezed, which set a family of foxes laughing.

"Creature, come down. I'll find us a roof to sleep on."

Creature leapt easily, 15 feet to the ground.

IN DAWN'S BLUE HOUR, Creature woke with a start and nearly toppled off the library roof. Mother was only just alert enough to catch them.

"What happened? Are you hurt?"

"Humans threw rocks at me."

Mother unfurled so that she doubled, then tripled in size. Peering down past the gutter line, she scanned the parking lot and the field behind it. Seeing no one, she forced her eyesight to sharpen focus. "Where are they?" she whispered.

"I don't know," Creature answered, pressing their body hard against Mother's leg. "I saw them with my eyes closed."

"When you were sleeping?"

Creature nodded.

"You had a nightmare," Mother said, marveling at how Creature cuddled close now. She sank to her haunches to pull them in close and pet them. Then she bit down on their neck wrinkles and glided them both down to the center courtyard, away from public view and on solid ground.

Creature rose to their feet clumsily and, unfamiliar with the breadth or capabilities of the new extensions to their body, dragged their new appendages over grass, plantings, and stonework.

"What are these? Get them off!" Creature shouted, violently thrashing in circles as if they'd been hornet stung.

"Calm down," Mother said, catching Creature before they could crash into stained glass windows. "You can't remove them. They're part of you now."

"I hate them. I don't want them."

"What is it you don't like?"

"No one else has them."

Mother pointed to her own wings. "We're just the same."

"No, we're not!"

At this stage, Creature's wings were thick as birch bark, while hers were snakeskin thin. "Yours are still growing," Mother explained.

Creature looked stricken. "You mean, they'll grow even larger than they are now?"

<hr>

ALL THE NEXT DAY, Creature hid in a leaf pile at the edge of the playground, a camouflaged cat reluctant to pounce. Sometimes a squirrel or chipmunk dropped by to chatter, and one time a dog sniffed the pile and Mother had to shoo them away when they lifted their leg.

The children stayed away though, and that made Creature angry. "They don't want to play with me!"

"You could come out of hiding," Mother suggested. "Humans are, generally speaking, oblivious. If you don't make yourself obvious, no one will know that you're here."

"I want them to look for me. But I don't want them to find me. They might throw rocks."

Mother thought it was fascinating, really, and also terribly sad that Creature wanted to be noticed, but not seen, at least not in their entirety. But then again, that's how their kind had survived for so long: by concealing aspects of themselves instead of showing the world who they truly are.

When at last the playground emptied, Mother said, "It's okay for you to come out now."

"Humans don't have wings," Creature stated.

"That's right," Mother said, "We look a lot like them, but we're different."

"Birds have wings. Are we birds?"

"No."

"Insects?"

"No."

"Are there others like us?"

"Yes, but not many." Mother wondered if that revelation made Creature feel lonely.

"I hate my wings. They're ugly."

"Come now, that's no way to talk about yourself," Mother said, then she gently bit down on Creature's scruff. She flew them to the wild fields to show Creature how to stain their wings with coreopsis and marigolds.

But Creature didn't like their wings stained purple and yellow. They angrily macerated acorns and sumac leaves, mixed the sludge with pond silt, then turned their wings black with mud and juice.

Mother did not take offense to Creature's experimentation. The colors would all fade quickly because Creature was growing quickly and would morph again soon.

CROWS WOKE MOTHER AT DAYBREAK, sounding their call of alarm. They told her Creature was making a terrible mess, binding their wings tight to their body with tent caterpillar webs.

"Where? Where are they?" Mother cried, desperate.

"In the forest," they squawked.

Mother flew there in an instant. A lunge, a grab, she held tight even as Creature tried to pull away. She used a talon to slice through layers of sticky thread so she could get a good look at what Creature hid: shredded skin on their back and shoulders, a mottled patch of blood and a bruise spreading wide.

"Who did this?" Mother demanded.

A third lid slid sideways over Creature's downcast eyes. "Mother, you're scaring me," they whimpered, which made Mother soften her stance, then her tone, then her grip on Creature's arm.

"Did you do this intentionally? Please, it's important. I need to know."

"If I didn't have these wings I'd look like a human."

Mother was horrified. "I understand wanting to fit in, Creature, but changing your appearance won't erase who you are."

THAT NIGHT, clouds heavy with storm water rolled in. Mother flew Creature to a slate-shingle roof atop a swaying, disused barn. She said, "We will spend the night here. We're not as high up as we were at the library." What she meant was, at this height, Creature would not hurt themself if they were startled by a crack of lightning and fell to the pillow of white clover below on the ground.

Creature circled the roof slant once, twice, then crouched and rested their chin on their knees, like Mother had taught them. Soon they closed their eyes.

When rain splattered, Mother unfurled her wings to shelter

Creature, but she need not have bothered. Even as Creature curled up sleeping, their own wings unfurled and curved around them in a protective shell. Yesterday's thick, stubby wings had matured into vitreous membranes, refracting moonlight into hundreds of halos bouncing off bark and leaf and flower, calling fireflies from their hiding places to light up the night sky.

"Creature hates their wings," Mother lamented to the ancient ones, hoping for illumination about how to change Creature's mind. Thrumming in her hollow bones meant the ancestors were listening, but her mouth gurgled rainwater too loud for her to hear their sage advice.

At daybreak, Mother saw a wood duck fly down from her nest in a tree hollow 68 feet above the ground. One by one, her flightless ducklings leapt from their nest to follow her to water. Every one of them landed unharmed.

Mother's gaze shifted to Creature whose open wounds had turned to scars overnight. She thanked the miracle of life for its healing powers and the ancient ones for their wisdom. Then she gently deposited sleeping Creature in the wood duck's abandoned nest.

After gathering a pile of leaves below the tree trunk, Mother called out. "Creature, wake up! A new day has dawned."

Creature's voice was muffled and pitched high inside that tree hole. "Mother? Where am I?"

"You're in a tree. I brought you here early this morning." Mother answered from below. "You can come down now."

Creature emerged from the hollow. They sank their nails into bark, turned this way and that and, awkwardly headfirst and sometimes sideways, began to climb down.

"No, not that way!" Mother scolded. "Spread your wings and jump!"

"It's too high. I can't do it," Creature replied. "I need you to come up here and help me down."

Mother and Creature went back and forth like that, accomplishing nothing, with Mother saying, "Jump," and Creature answering, "I can't," until finally bark came loose from phloem compelling Creature's cries to grow more plaintive, and Mother decided she needed to end their argument before Creature lost their grip and came tumbling down.

Mother met Creature in the branches.

Only this time, she did not bite down on Creature's scruff to carry them.

Nor pull Creature close to protect them.

This time, instead, Mother pushed.

HE WILL MAKE HIS OWN LUCK

MARK FIGLOZZI

A pair of bronze-age newlyweds wrestles with destiny and a giant squid one stormy night on the Mediterranean.

Mark Figlozzi was born in a small town in northern New York, where there are more cows than people. He studied writing at Oberlin, screenwriting in LA, and is the creative director of a design agency in Seattle.

PLAYLIST

Keep You Safe — **The Crane Wives**
Lie In Our Graves — **Dave Matthews Band**
Menwith Hill — **The Chevin**
Romeo and Juliet (Dire Straits Cover) — **Widowspeak**
Come Alive — **Madonna**
Ballerina — **Van Morrison**
Stoned at the Nail Salon — **Lorde**
Follow Me Home — **Dire Straits**

Scan to listen at buttonhall.com/books/left-turns

The fisherman leaned out over the side of his whale-skin canoe and lowered his torch toward the dark water. He had rolled the torch in black powder to make it hiss and smoke and shoot sparks in the night. This would lure her to the surface.

With his other hand he raised his spear. Tip steady, pointed at the sea. The shaft rested on his bare shoulder. In this state of muscular suspension—waiting, poised to kill—he had spent the entire day. He ached.

Come and look at the pretty fire, he whispered. *How can you resist?*

Back in Amnisos, his young wife would be waiting for him by the cookfire. Naeema would have a stew on the hearth and their little cottage would be thick with the mingled scents of leeks and clams, peppers and saffron. Naeema's skin would be fire-warm. They were three moons married, trying to make a baby, and tonight, she had told him, would be the night.

"Be home by dusk," she'd teased, "and I will make it worth your while."

Now the sky sang with stars.

He glanced back over his shoulder. Across the bay the pale cliffs shone cold in the moonlight. Beneath them, the docks of Amnisos jutted out into the Mediterranean. Their familiar outlines shimmered against the sea as the dock-fires burned low.

The sea churned beneath the whale-skin canoe. A constellation of silver bubbles flickered up from the depths and burst against the surface.

He lowered his torch toward the oily water. Was something there?

ALL WINTER he had shadowed the giant octopus, Circoth. She hunted at dusk. She flew from her den beneath Black Crow Rock on a silent jet of water, gliding through canyons of coral. She trailed her tentacles behind her, a kestrel of the watery skies. Glory awaited the man whose spear-tip plunged through her eye —if he could drag her carcass back to the docks at Amnisos.

In a dream, the Goddess had promised him Circoth. When he woke, he built a spear like the one she'd shown him. He carved its shaft from True Oak, hollowed it out and shot through its core a vein of copper. On its barbed hook he etched the shape of Circoth's eye. He named the spear for her: *Circoth-Naq*.

Last night his young bride had turned away from him. She stood in the doorway and gazed up at the white mountain. A luminous cloud trailed across the sky — the lights of far-off Knossos. Some said it was the smoke of ten thousand cookfires.

Naeema turned to face him, a challenge in her eyes. "You love that monster more than me!"

"I love her, my wife," he whispered, savoring the word *wife*, holding it on his lips as though it were a kiss. "I love her," he said, "but not more than you." And then he proved it.

Before dawn he slipped out of the cottage and down to the west dock, where the humblest boats of leather and vine knocked together in the mist. He knelt beside his whale-skin canoe to untie a knot and heard a whisper behind him.

"Husband." Naeema regarded him with dark eyes. "Bring me a boatful of tuna."

"Tonight, I bring you something better." He rose and

touched her cheek. "When I come home, I will be famous. Not ordinary —"

"You were never ordinary —"

"And then you and I can go anywhere. When I have killed Circoth, no one can stop us. We'll sail away and be free of this place. We will make our own luck."

"No one can make their own luck."

"Have faith." He kissed her, and her lips tasted of sea-salt. "Don't fear."

Naeema looked out at the sea, considered a moment. At last she sighed. "It's the season for storms. Come back before dark—"

"I will."

"Or if the weather changes."

"I will."

"And swear this to me." She squeezed his hand. "Do not sail into Thera's shadow."

"I swear it. I swear to Sky Father Bull."

"*Him?*" She shook her head. "The Bull doesn't care about you or me. Swear to the Goddess."

"I swear to the Goddess," he laughed, "I will not sail into Thera's shadow."

Then without a word she turned toward home. Barefoot she padded along the dock, then across the sand. Why did he feel so heartsick? This very night he would return to her awash in Circoth's glory and they would make a baby. A son, maybe. And no ordinary fisherman's boy.

A CRACK of thunder split the sky. He fumbled his spear and nearly dropped it. Had he dozed? The torch was out.

He could no longer see the distant lights of Amnisos on the

water. Even the stars were gone. Where had the current carried him?

Somewhere beneath him, the sea moved. There was something down there. He gripped the canoe's frame, peered down at the water.

Something brushed the bottom of the boat. Long, slow and smooth, a slithering finger stroked the length of his keel.

Circoth was slipping away! He raised his spear and knelt against the side of the boat. Muscles tense, body taut. Ready for the kill.

"Show yourself."

A cold wind blew across his bow.

A fork of lightning split the night. In the flash of light he saw her — an aquatic eye gazing lamplike from the depths. He raised his spear but it was dark again.

Another flash — something towered over him in the dark, a shadow against the sky. A vast, black mountainside. Silent stones radiated cold in the dark: the shadow of Thera.

Heart pounding, he dropped the spear into the bottom of the boat and grabbed the oar. He thrust its tip into the sea and spun the canoe around. With the forbidden isle at his back now, he began to paddle toward home and Naeema.

He shook, but only from hunger. Exhaustion, perhaps, but not fear. Not fear.

"I am sorry, Naeema."

The mountain sighed, a cold breath at the back of his neck. Behind him, the hiss of rain on the sea.

He paddled hard, searching the horizon for the lights of Amnisos. Blood pounded in his ears. The storm raced toward him.

Sky Father Bull, he whispered, rowing hard. *Don't take me tonight! — Let me see her again. Just one more time. Let me hold Naeema.*

But it was a fool's prayer. He had nothing to offer the Bull.

The rain swept over him, a rage against his bare shoulders. Icy fingers down his spine. He paddled harder.

Seawater flooded in. It sloshed around his feet. Daggers of rain slashed his face. His fingers on the oar grew raw and pink till at last the oar slipped from his grasp.

He heard it splash down in the canoe.

He fell forward, grasping for it. He gulped bilgewater, spat ice and blood. Numb fingers came up empty.

The sea lit up around him. The sky gods leapt from Thera's mountaintop and thundered across the sky. They towered over him, tearing up the sea. The waves frothed. No way forward.

He fumbled for the oar. "I will give up Circoth and stay ashore!" He heard himself shout.

He rose to his knees in the icy water, stared up into the rain.

"I will remain in Amnisos." His voice faltered. "I will try to be content—a tuna fisherman—but let me survive this night."

He felt his spear beneath him. He needed an oar, but *Circoth-Naq* floated between his knees.

"Is this your price?" Tears welled in his eyes.

Floating in the bilgewater, the spear began to ring. It vibrated against the hull with a deep, metallic hum. It sang the song of a spear. It called to him.

"Then I accept. Take my spear. Make me an *ordinary* man— make me *nobody*—but Sky Father, let me hold Naeema again!"

He seized the spear, clambered to his feet. He raised it over his head and thrust it into the sky. The sky gods blazed before him. The rain lashed his face. The boat lurched beneath him, taking on water.

"We will make a son," he whispered. Let *him* grow up proud. Let *him* sail away and be free of this place. "Naeema!" he cried. "I am coming home to you!"

The sky gods hurled a bolt of power. *Crack!* His spear was a weathervane pointed at heaven. *Crack!* His fist locked around the shaft. The air ignited. His skeleton rang in perfect resonance with the luminous sea.

And he began to rise. Back arched, arms upstretched, lifted on light, his mortal blood boiled away in his veins, distilled to the immortal ichor of the gods. His skin steamed. His teeth cracked in his skull. He grinned. He would ride this wave of power away from here. Sit with the sky gods, choose a throne, drink from their cups. He would reach down and raise Naeema beside him. Show her how to fly on a ray of light. They would leave this place and go to the sky together.

The heavenly light extinguished. The sky gods released him, and he fell.

He splashed back into his half-sunk canoe, lay in cold water. His body crackled with energy, twitching, until the power discharged and cold rain flowed over his gray lips.

A flurry of ash rained down. The blackened canoe drifted, cold, through a patch of steaming sea.

Silver fish churned up from the depths and floated on the surface.

A vast, black form floated up from the abyss. For a moment, until the wind changed, its long tentacles drifted, lifeless, around the blackened canoe. Touching it, almost.

***

"Naeema!" She dropped her candle and ran across the sand.

A few stars shone through the broken clouds. The black shore glittered with pebbles of ice.

The men had gathered at the water's edge. She could see their torches. When they recognized her, they fell silent and looked at her with firelit faces. She shoved them aside, charged into icy water.

"Naeema, wait."

She felt a hand on her shoulder, brushed it away and waded deeper, beyond the torches into the dark water where other men splashed and shouted, dragging something from the sea. A knotted net? A fallen tree? But her heart knew. She had known all day.

He lay on his back in the blackened canoe. He was smiling, eyes turned toward the sky.

"My husband!" She dove into the canoe, but he was heavy, his skin icy. Gray like the flesh of a beached jellyfish.

The canoe rocked beneath her as the men dragged it onto the sand.

She brushed a finger across his lips. So cold.

The priestesses circled the boat, red cloaks against the night. Now they reached for her.

"No!" She wrapped herself around him. "Tonight was our night. The Goddess heard our promise!"

With bony fingers they grabbed her. They locked gnarled hands on her wrists and ankles. She lashed out as they tore her from her husband's body.

She heard the angry hiss of the whale-skin canoe as the men dragged him away across the sand. The priestesses hissed, tongues in teeth, trying to mask the sound but she knew the weight of him. She knew the sound of his boat on sand.

"Child," said the eldest. "You must be strong."

She was. Like a wildcat she convulsed — got her leg free and kicked one of them — but the others forced her down, laid her back in the sand. Pressed her down. All of them in crimson cloaks, they knelt upon her till she could scarcely breathe. Stiff and wet and pressed against the sand, Naeema stopped fighting.

"Please." She heard her voice break. "We were only just married."

"Hush," they cooed. "He is gone now. Be strong." They

caressed her body with bony fingers, ran long nails gently over her scalp, combing her tangled hair.

She watched a bat fluttering overhead, black against the stars. Back and forth it flew, out to sea and back again. Out to sea and back again.

***

THE COTTAGE WAS QUIET. The embers of a great fire burned down to molten cores and cracked on the hearth. Everything glowed in deep firelight: the rough clay walls, the young bride, and her husband's corpse. Shadows in motion cast an illusion of life.

She'd laid him on the bench. Now she knelt before him and touched his pale cheek. She traced his collarbone with her thumb, laid her palms on his bare chest. Here beside her fire his skin grew warm again.

From the coals, a black pot rattled and hissed. Its smoke-stained copper handle jutted out over the flames.

Long ago Naeema's grandmother had come to Amnisos from the highland groves. She had taught Naeema how to make many kinds of tea. This particular brew turned red when it reached a boil. Naeema had filled the small copper pot to its brim. Every drop counted.

She breathed deep the mingled scents of saffron and garlic, frankincense and holy mandrake.

The red liquid burbled and splashed over the rim. A drop hit the handle and hissed away to nothing.

Naeema raised her right hand, looked down at her open palm. She looked at the pot. Felt her body rock with the pounding of her heart.

Now, she thought. *Before fear stops me.*

She braced herself. "Goddess," she whispered, "I offer you flesh: mine for his."

And she reached over the fire and seized the pot's handle.

A blaze of pain seared her palm and she cried out, fighting the urge to drop the pot. The handle seared her skin. She staggered back, held steady. A moan escaped her lips.

Do not spill it.

The red tea rolled and hissed against the pot, and the vibrating pot screamed against her palm. Pain pounded with every heartbeat. The cottage reeked of burning meat.

She knelt over her husband. With her left forefinger she parted his cold lips. She wriggled her finger between his teeth, pried them apart and poured a few drops of red tea into his grey mouth. It bubbled away down his throat, turned his grey tongue pink.

Quickly she turned away, and leaning over the hearth she replaced the pot among the coals. Her head swam, palm throbbed. When she turned back to her husband, she screamed.

He shook — sat up, clutched his throat. A hideous rasp escaped his lungs, and he covered his mouth. Then he lay back on the bench, peaceful. Blinking.

He took a deep breath and he said, "Something smells delicious."

She knelt beside him. Tears welled in her eyes. *Not now,* she thought, blinking them away. *Do not waste these moments.*

He looked up at her. "Is it tonight?" His skin glowed red from the fire. "You said tonight, didn't you?"

Doesn't he know what has happened? Does he not remember?

He sat up, swung his legs over the bench and rested his feet on the floor. "What's the matter, Naeema? Did you burn yourself?"

"Yes." She sobbed. *My sweet husband.* "Yes, husband. Tonight."

She glanced back over her shoulder at the pot. Her hearth was so hot. The tea would not last long there. It was already seething and bubbling again. Soon it would boil away to nothing and then all would grow cold again.

Yet even so, now she turned to face him and found she could not bring herself to touch him. What power had touched him? What power lived in him now?

She shook.

He rose. His red skin steamed in the firelight. He stood over her, reached down to touch her and she cringed. She scrambled to her feet, backed away toward the fire. Only his burning fingertips grazed her forearm. He looked at her, hurt.

"Naeema." His voice cracked. "I am sorry."

"Sorry?" Tears welled in her eyes. "Why?"

"I am sorry," he whispered, "I sailed too far."

"You fool," she said, trying for a laugh, but it broke as it passed her lips and came out a sob.

No time to fall to pieces. She forced a smile. *We have never had time.*

Trembling, she slipped her right hand beneath the hem of her skirt. She did not want him to see her palm, not now. With her left hand she reached for him.

He took her hand, his fingers hot. She stepped toward him. His skin smelled of storms and woodsmoke.

He pressed his face against hers, forehead to forehead, hot breath rasping over his parted lips. "Don't be angry."

"Never," she whispered. "Never."

She blinked hard. And in that dark instant she dreamed they would live their whole lives together. She dreamed they would sail together, whisper secrets, raise children, grow old. She dreamed they would plant a garden, argue about small things. Waste days; entire days. She dreamed they would live whole lives together; days and nights uncounted. And then she opened her eyes and she kissed him.

His mouth was hot. His lips, his tongue. His breath like fire.

Now he placed his burning palms on the back of her neck. Slid down to the small of her back and untied her skirt. It fell to the floor. The cookfire blazed against the backs of her legs, grandmother's red tea boiling away to nothing.

He brushed a hot fingertip over her cheek, traced her eyebrow while he gently parted her knees with his and moved into her space till all her world was his body, hot —blazing hot, everywhere against her. She opened her mouth and he was there. Softly she hissed. Hot steam flowed over her skin.

His burning hands linked behind the small of her back, slid down until he could lift her. Her feet left the floor. She gasped. He burned against her thighs.

She blinked back the rising tears, whispered his name and opened herself to him. Here by the hearth they rose and fell together like the flames beneath the tea pot.

High on the cliffside a bonfire leapt up. The priestesses beat the holy drums and flames leapt into the night. Down by the caves the sea pounded the rocky shore, devouring sand, licking crevices. The tide came in and set a sea full of empty fishing boats rocking and bumping against the docks, bound together by knotted ropes that snapped and smoked as the waves heaved them against each other.

On the hearth an ember burst. A spark of lightning exploded from him into her. And where it touched Naeema, the spark of life kindled. And she knotted her fingers in his hair and cried out his name. She pushed him down and together they fell to the floor.

All of Amnisos, hearing her voice, believed that Naeema had finally realized her husband was dead.

He lay beneath her, breathing deep.

She draped herself over him, buried him in frantic kisses. It would not be long now. *Doesn't he know?*

He reached up and ran his fingers through her tangled hair. "Naeema," he said. "Naeema."

His eyes closed. She touched his luminous cheek and burned her fingertips.

Outside there came a low roll of thunder, the memory of a storm. A great sob rose within her. She swallowed it, choked it down. *Not yet. Please Goddess, not yet.*

"My Husband." She lay upon him, pressed her cheek against his sweat-slick breast and listened to the rise and fall of his breath, rhythmic as the sea. She shut her eyes and felt the drumbeat of his heart against her cheek. It pounded like a galloping horse racing home, thunderous and exhausted from a long day's hunt.

And then it stopped.

IN THE FALL, it was the screaming of a baby that brought the neighbors to Naeema's house.

They stopped in the doorway.

Ecchi the fisherwoman shook her head as the others packed in behind her. *Poor girl.*

No one had even known Naeema was pregnant. She'd carried the baby in secret all this time beneath her mourning cloak. Ecchi clucked her tongue. Naeema had been stronger, even, than they knew.

Now she lay dead on her own muddy floor, cold arms still wrapped around a howling infant. He was a newborn boy — small, like his dead mother — but surely worth something to someone. He flushed a healthy pink when he screamed.

Pushing through the doorway, the grandmothers clucked

and shook their heads. "Always going her own way. Never asking no one for help."

"It's not her fault." Ecchi rounded on them. She was childless. She was younger than the others but not so young that she still dared hope. "The girl did fine. It was her luck that changed. The gods are with you till one day they aren't." She wagged her finger. "It could happen to anyone."

She bent down, scooped up the infant and wrapped him in the fold of her dress. Feeling the thrum of his tiny life against her, she forgot the others. The baby stopped wailing and looked at her. His little chest convulsed with the echoes of sobs. His eyes were the darkest blue like a storm at sea. Strange, dark eyes like his father's. But there was something different, too.

Ecchi said, "I'm taking him."

The others gasped.

She shrugged. "If he's anything like his parents, he'll grow into a handsome thing. Clever, too."

"What good will that do him?" said one of the grandmothers. She scowled at the dried blood on the floor, the dried wedding flowers hung upside down over the window. "An evil fate is written here."

"Hush, witch," Ecchi hissed. "She was unlucky."

The grandmother shrugged. She knelt beside the dead girl, closed Naeema's eyes and tried to wipe the blood from her cheek. "Poor thing."

"But *he's* alive," Ecchi said. "Aren't you, child!" His little fists clenched. "Yes, you are. And so there is hope for you."

Outside, an echo of distant thunder rumbled across the bay. The last storm of the season was gathering. The infant turned his head at the sound, and craned his neck, looking toward the sky.

Ecchi smiled. Such strength in his tiny fingers. "Evil fate, *pheh*. This one will never be drawn to the sea." She rocked him.

"Doesn't need the likes of *you* telling him where he can go or what he can do."

"The gods will do that for him," grumbled the grandmother.

"No they won't!" Ecchi snapped. "I will name him Daedalus."

"*Maker?*" The grandmother laughed. "What will he make?"

"I told you." She cradled the infant in her arms, looked down at him and spoke softly, just the whisper of a song: "Daedalus will make his own luck."

He kicked against her, looked up at her with those dark eyes. She felt a fire inside him, as though he burned with the heat of the sun. It made her smile.

THE BIG CRUNCH
LORIN OBERWEGER

An elementary school science teacher has all the answers for their students but is at a loss to explain why their true love seems to be slipping away.

An award-winning author, Lorin Oberweger has eight traditionally published books (five fiction, three nonfiction), including BOOMERANG, REBOUND, and BOUNCE, published by Harper/William Morrow. Her latest is THANK YOU FOR COMING TO MY TED TALK, written with TED director, Chris Anderson.

Lorin is also a highly sought-after independent book editor and ghostwriter with more than twenty-five years experience in publishing. Her company, Free Expressions, offers writing workshops nationwide, and she's known for her one-on-one story mastermind work.

PLAYLIST

Space Oddity — **David Bowie**
Spaceman — **The Killers**
Who's Loving You — **Jennie Lind**
Gravel — **Ani DiFranco**
Blood in the Cut — **K Flay**
Every Breath You Take — **The Police**
There's a Star for Everyone — **Aretha Franklin**

Scan to listen at buttonhall.com/books/left-turns

t doesn't help that you are drunk.

It doesn't even help that she's drunk too and that the night sky is littered with stars and the breeze smells of jasmine.

It doesn't help that you can tell her the difference between a singularity and a wormhole, that you can point out Canis Minor, that even in your compromised condition you can recite Pi to the thirtieth digit. None of it, not even your storehouse of arcane knowledge, seems to be doing the trick tonight.

The two of you sway together, trashed on margaritas, in a bar parking lot. You have already forgotten which bar. You are leaning against a car—not your own—and you are kissing. You have been kissing for what seems like hours, breathing tequila into each other's mouths. Unfortunately, though you wish it were otherwise, you are not too drunk to notice that something is missing.

You pull her closer, renew your efforts. You imagine there is a white light pulsing within you, down in your solar-plexus. At first a dull throb, it evolves into something more acute. It is as light and translucent as a bubble. It rises within you. You feel it, floating up from your belly, warm in your throat. Then it is in your mouth and too full, too round and almost bursting, to keep to yourself. So you let it go. You let it go and tongue love into her mouth.

But she rejects it, parrying your love with the artful paddle of her tongue. She pulls away, and her necklace catches on your shirt button. You disentangle yourselves, and she leans back against the car door. She brushes the back of her hand across her lips and regards you for a long, crushing moment. Then she laughs and pulls you closer, pressing cool lips against yours.

Though she clings to you now and utters those devastating little moans, you know that the sex you will have later on, peeling off your clothes before you've even made it to her bedroom, will be an act. You know you can never really penetrate.

IN THE CLASSROOM the next day you attempt to teach the Big Bang Theory to twenty wiggling fifth graders. You talk about stable and unstable particles, about protons and neutrons. You talk, in general terms, about the cosmological principle. You say that the universe was thought to be infinite, but that now there is a question of whether this is so. You do the kids a favor and spare them the Big Crunch, knowing that any talk of the universe swallowing itself back up again will give some of these kids nightmares for a month. Even telling them it won't happen in their lifetimes or in their great-great-great-great grandchildren's lifetimes won't help. It didn't help you when you learned about it.

For a moment, your animation seizes the students and holds them rapt. Their mouths slightly agape, they follow your every movement as you pace in front of your desk. You tap the blackboard with your long wooden pointer. You draw invisible galaxies in the air, waving the pointer like a maestro. The kids are right there with you, watching, responding. They ask questions. Good ones. You think perhaps your stick waving has had a hypnotic effect on them. But no, you realize, it just might be that they're learning something.

YOU FIND IT FUNNY, in a heart-bruising way, that the things that drew you so powerfully to her in the beginning are the things that now dig at you, wreck your sleep. You liked her straightforward manner, the way she met you square-on, without any of the self-deprecation or psychic batting of eyelashes you'd found in other women. You realize now that loving her is like loving a photocopy. It looks the same, but it's one step removed.

Take now, for instance. She stands next to you at her kitchen counter, telling you jokes while you chop vegetables for dinner.

"You have carrot on your shirt," she says, and hands you a dishtowel. She slips an arm around your back and kisses your shoulder.

This is the problem. She does all the right things. She keeps you company in the kitchen, reads to you from the newspaper. It's not that she doesn't feel. You know she does. It's just that you can't feel her feeling. Her emotions seem to radiate from her and then stop short, as though they've reached a force field of some kind, an impenetrable barrier around her. Or around you. It's hard to tell, and at some point the whole thing becomes too esoteric for you to follow.

When she leaves to go buy some wine for dinner, you do something stupid. You enter her office, a place that while not officially off-limits, has always seemed verboten. In fact you're surprised to find that the door is unlocked.

You look at her desk, at her computer and stacks of books. Everything is orderly. Her pencil sharpener, tape dispenser, hole punch and stapler form a neat row on the edge of her desk. Reference books line one entire shelf and you are not surprised to find they're in alphabetical order by title.

On one wall is a series of black and white photographs of women with their nude backs turned toward the viewer. Slender women, heavy ones, muscular ones.

You sit at her computer, listen for the sound of the front door opening. You call up her word processor and pick a file at random. As you begin to read, something sinks inside you. What she writes is not what you expect, which is something trenchant and literary, something that Joyce Carol Oates would review in "The New York Review of Books." Instead, you find yourself in the dark cyberpunk world of her imagination, on a weapons run with a bold, riot-grrl heroine (whose mechanical heart causes you to emit a sharp, pained laugh) and a flinty-eyed hero who— blonde-haired and taciturn—is, quite clearly, not you.

You don't bother to read on. You shut down the program, push back the chair, get up and move toward the door. You touch things as you go, like a blind man in need of tactile guidance.

You make it out in plenty of time. In fact, she takes long enough with the wine for you to look through her bills and stand inside her bedroom closet for a full five minutes. You don't know what you're looking for there, but whatever it is, it's not to be found within the rows of neatly-hung clothes, all in lifeless pastels quite unbefitting a riot-grrl.

You breathe in the slight powdery scent and flash on the idea of trying on one of her blouses. Shaken, you exit her closet in a hurry.

Over dinner you ask her to tell you something about herself. Something that no one else knows. Something shocking. You used to be able to draw her out this way, one enticing morsel at a time.

"But I'm so simple," she protests, laughing. "There's nothing to tell." She bunches the tablecloth in one hand, then releases it. There is a long pause before you realize that's all she's going to say. You decide that what she really means is, "You're so simple. Too simple to understand my complicated and enigmatic nature."

You extricate yourself as quickly as possible after dinner. You find yourself vanishing in her good-bye kiss and disappear completely as the door shuts behind you.

YOU TAKE the kids to the local planetarium. They are enthralled, just as you hoped they would be. You tilt back in your seat and look up at the domed cosmos.

Constellations tick into formation above you. The planetarium's director—a young guy with wispy, mad scientist hair—patiently takes your kids through the signs of the Zodiac. One of the kids comments that it'd be easy to find Ursa Minor in real life too, if only it had a big, red arrow pointing to it like it does here. The name Cassiopeia makes them giggle.

"The light we see has traveled millions of years across the galaxy," he tells the group. "Sometimes, by the time we see it, the stars no longer exist."

You realize that this is what it feels like with her. That what you get from her is like the dead-light from an extinct star.

In the quiet, one of the kids says, "Where did stars come from?"

"From God, dummy," says another.

A moment, then: "Well, who made God?"

There is a hush while they consider that. You hold your breath, knowing you can't shield them from what will be a natural progression. From God, they will turn to questions of their own existences, to the mystery of life and death, to their places in the world and their own quests to mold order out of chaos. You can't spare them the puzzle and the surreal moments they have before them. You know in your heart that even if you could, you shouldn't.

ONE NIGHT, the two of you lie in bed, watching "To Kill a Mockingbird" on cable. You're embarrassed to admit it, but the part where Atticus walks out of the courtroom after losing his case always gets to you.

The moment comes and goes and as always, you get a little emotional. Just the requisite burning in the throat and a couple of fat tears that plop onto your T-shirt and soak in.

The movie ends. You look over at her and smile sheepishly. She returns a thin smile, but her eyes are dry.

"What did you think?" you ask.

She removes her glasses and sets them carefully down on the bedside table. "I've seen it before."

"Doesn't the end..."

"I don't know." She shrugs. "It feels like manipulation. Like the end of "It's a Wonderful Life.""

So, you begin stalking her.

Only you don't call it that to yourself. You are simply...what? Keeping apprised of her whereabouts. That's all. You tell yourself this is not you. You are a trusted teacher. A registered voter, for God's sake. The one thing you definitely are not is a stalker.

And yet, here you are, standing outside her building in a drizzling rain. You shudder beneath the portico, stepping forward every now and then to look at her apartment, three stories up. This is crazy, you think. You feel like a cliché or like a character in a bad film. You could simply ask her what she does with her time away from you or what it is she feels deeply about. Perhaps you're afraid of the answer, afraid to find out that deep inside her is as black and cold as space.

Finally, against every notion of what you consider rational behavior, you move away from the sheltered doorway and begin the long climb up to her fire escape. The metal rungs are wet and slimy beneath your hands. You can barely hold on.

Then you are there, on the balcony outside her bedroom window. You work on catching your breath. The lights are on. You see her through the sheer curtains, sitting on the edge of the bed, hunched over, her face in her hands. After a moment you notice that her shoulders are shaking. She is crying.

Thunder reverberates in the distance, but you barely hear it. You wipe rain from the window so you can get a better look. How foolish you were to think she had no feelings! For all you know she is sitting in there, crying over the fact that you haven't called her in days. Of course, she doesn't know you've been busy spying on her, but that's probably just as well.

You are about to turn away, to rush down so you can find a place to call her, when a shadow falls over her and a man steps into the room. He leans against the wall, folds his arms across his chest. He is tall and blond and looks...taciturn. Your brain freezes. Anxiety swells inside you, an ice flower blooming in your chest.

She dries her eyes with the back of her hand, then rises from the bed and goes to him. She tries to put her arms around his neck, but he catches them and places them back down by her side. His expression is stony, unyielding. She crumples then, onto the carpet, her long hair swinging forward, hiding her face. She sobs—you can actually hear it—and grabs fistfuls of the mauve throw rug.

Lightning flashes. Startled, you pitch forward and smack against the window, then fall onto the iron grating like a dazed pigeon. You get blearily to your feet and see that the man is at the window, struggling to get it open. He yells something. You rush to the ladder and start down.

Close to the bottom, you lose your balance. Your feet skid out from under you like a cartoon character's—pinwheeling—and you slip, smashing your chin against the ladder.

You see stars.

When you come to, your girlfriend's lover is kneeling over you, gently slapping your face. "Are you all right?" he asks. Up close you see that he is even more chiseled and Nordic than you feared.

You push his hands away, struggle to sit up.

"What were you doing up there?" His voice is kind, which of course makes it worse.

What can you say? "I'm sorry," is the only thing that seems appropriate.

He helps you to your feet and you begin a slow limp off into the night. As you pass the building's portico, you see her standing there. She steps out into the light and looks at you. There is something in her expression, an emotion. For the first time ever, you feel it truly reach you.

Unfortunately, it's pity.

It is the last moment of the last day of school. The children cluster around your desk to watch you open the present they have chipped in to buy you. It is a globe of the night sky. You plug it in and the stars glow. There is something impossibly poignant about their expressions when you thank them for their kindness. You tell them they are your favorite students ever and they duck their heads and blush.

You take time to praise each child individually. This one for taking care of the class iguana. That one for resolving conflict among her friends. You think of adding a quote from Oscar Wilde: "We are all of us in the gutter, but some of us are looking at the stars," but decide it's a little heavy for eleven-year-olds.

The bell rings, and the scraping of sneakers against linoleum is almost deafening. The children rush to their cubbyholes to collect their supplies. Then they rush out the door, calling out their good-byes as they go and toppling a chair in the process.

You right it then step out into the hallway to watch the procession.

The students race down the hall. They jostle each other as they go, riding up on each other's heels. They laugh the kind of laughter that only comes at the beginning of summer.

"Order!" you shout after them.

But you know they will grow up and do what grown-ups do: choose chaos every time.